Outside the palace walls

Misha turned down a narrow street and slowed to my pace, taking hold of my arm. There were dreary-looking factories set among the homes. Misha turned into one of them.

I was amazed to see that most of the workers were boys and girls, some of them younger than I was. "Why are there so many children?" I asked.

"Their wages are low. They'll work all day for next to nothing."

"And when school starts again?"

"This is their school. This is what they learn."

By now some of the children had noticed us and paused in their work to stare. One of them was a girl who looked my age. I started to walk toward her, thinking to speak to her, but two inspectors noticed us. Quickly Misha pulled me out into the street.

"For once, Katya, you have nothing to say."

I didn't.

ALSO BY GLORIA WHELAN

THE IMPOSSIBLE JOURNEY

FRUITLANDS:
Louisa May Alcott Made Perfect

HOMELESS BIRD

INDIAN SCHOOL

MIRANDA'S LAST STAND

The Island Trilogy:

ONCE ON THIS ISLAND

FAREWELL TO THE ISLAND

RETURN TO THE ISLAND

GLORIA WHELAN

ANGEL ON THE SQUARE

HARPERTROPHY®
AN IMPRINT OF HARPERCOLLINSPUBLISHERS

Harper Trophy® is a registered trademark of
HarperCollins Publishers Inc.

Angel on the Square
Copyright © 2001 by Gloria Whelan

Library of Congress Cataloging-in-Publication Data
Whelan, Gloria.
  Angel on the square / Gloria Whelan.
    p. cm.
  Summary: In 1913 Russia, twelve-year-old Katya eagerly
anticipates leaving her St. Petersburg home, though not her
older cousin Misha, to join her mother, a lady-in-waiting in
the household of Tsar Nicholas II, but the ensuing years
bring world war, revolution, and undreamed-of changes to
her life.
  ISBN 0-06-029030-7 — ISBN 0-06-029031-5 (lib. bdg.)
  ISBN 0-06-440879-5 (pbk.)
  1. Russia—History—Nicholas II, 1894–1917—Juvenile
fiction. [1. Russia—History—Nicholas II, 1894–1917—
Fiction. 2. Nicholas II, Emperor of Russia, 1868–1918—
Family—Fiction. 3. Revolutions—Fiction. 4. Saint
Petersburg (Russia)—Fiction.] I. Title.
PZ7.W5718 An   2001   2001016639
[Fic]—dc21   CIP
                                                 AC

Typography by Alison Donalty
11 12 13   LP/CW   10
❖
First Harper Trophy edition, 2003

Visit us on the World Wide Web!
www.harperchildrens.com

for Pat and Gus

ANGEL ON THE SQUARE

CHAPTER ONE

ST. PETERSBURG

Winter 1913

I could feel the crowd holding its breath, awaiting the moment when Tsar Nikolai II and Empress Alexandra would arrive. On this February day all of St. Petersburg was celebrating three hundred years of rule by the Romanov Tsars. How I longed to be with Mama. As a special friend of the Empress, she was already in the cathedral. I burrowed deeper into my fur-lined coat to escape the winter winds that swept across Russia all the way from icy Siberia. The soft warmth of the coat curled around me like a friendly cat. From the balcony of our mansion Misha and I looked across St. Petersburg's main avenue, the Nevsky Prospekt, to the Kazan Cathedral. The cathedral's two wings seemed to gather in all of St. Petersburg.

Imperial carriages and shiny black chauffeured automobiles rolled up to the cathedral's entrance. Grand dukes in military uniform and grand duchesses in court gowns and diamond tiaras stepped onto the red carpet.

The city of St. Petersburg itself was dressed in an ermine robe of snow, its frozen river and canals glittering like the duchesses' diamonds. In the distance the sun shone on the brightly colored domes of the Church of the Resurrection. "Look, Misha," I said, "The domes look like a tumble of crown jewels."

He scowled. "You are a romantic child, Katya. When I look at that church, what I see is Alexander's blood."

"Misha, that was years ago," I scolded. The church was built on the spot where Tsar Alexander II, Tsar

Nikolai's grandfather, had been assassinated. When Mama was only a baby, she witnessed the terrible scene. Her papa held her up to see Tsar Alexander only seconds before the bomb went off. Even now, after so many years, she trembled when she told the story. "No one thinks of such things now," I said, but Misha's expression did not change. Misha would not let himself be happy. He was cheerful only when he was worrying himself to death.

Misha, whose proper name was Mikhail Sergeyevich Gnedich, was sixteen and thought he was a man. He attended the Tenishev School and lived with us, for his mama was my mama's dearest friend, as close to Mama as a sister. Misha's papa died bravely for Russia in a naval battle in faraway Manchuria. His mama died soon after of typhoid, though some said it was of a broken heart. When I was four, my own papa died in that war. Though Mama was very sad, she did not die like Misha's mother.

Misha was tall. He was also thin, and he looked as

though he did not eat much, which was not true, because he ate all the time. He took such large portions, the footman who served him had to fight to keep a smile from his face. Misha had blond hair, which he smoothed down with water to tame the curls, so he always looked like he just came out of a bath.

The naughty thing about Misha was that he was forever criticizing our beloved Tsar, which made everyone furious with him. Once Mama sent Misha away from the table for blaming the Tsar for the war in which his papa and my papa died.

Afterward, when I stole upstairs to Misha's room to take him food, Misha said, "It is time the Tsar let the people decide for themselves what is best for their country."

"You are wrong," I said. "How can the people decide when they are uneducated and ignorant?"

Misha asked angrily, "Whose fault is it that they are uneducated?"

I told Misha that the Tsar, whom everyone called

"*Tsar-batyushev*," "little father," was God's representative on earth and must surely know what was best for Russia. Misha's ideas were dangerous, and I worried that they would get him into trouble.

Now Misha turned away from the balcony. "I'm going down into the street with the people," he said, and added in a sarcastic tone, "I want to hear what they are saying on this glorious occasion."

"Misha, take me with you," I coaxed.

"With your fancy clothes and your furs?" He shook his head.

"Wait a moment," I pleaded. "I'll borrow something from the servants' hall."

The servants were all at the windows watching the ceremony, so it was a simple thing to snatch an old wool cloak from its peg and slip away unseen. It must have belonged to a cook, because it smelled of onions and vinegar. There was little warmth in the cloak, for the wool was worn and thin.

Misha gave me one of his disapproving looks when

I returned. "You must always have your own way, Katya. Your mother spoils you." That taunt was an old story with Misha. I paid no attention but followed him out a side door, hurrying to keep up, for he was stalking on ahead, pretending not to know me.

I had been on the Nevsky Prospekt hundreds of times, but always with Mama or my governess, Lidya. Never before had I seen such crowds. When I finally caught up, I hung on to Misha. As the people pressed against me, I whispered to him, "They smell."

Under his breath Misha hissed, "They have no soap, and for that matter how much water can you carry up four flights of stairs?"

"Everyone has water in their houses," I protested.

"You are a fool, Katya. You know nothing of the world." He shook off my hand and pushed his way to the front of the crowd. The sun disappeared behind dark clouds. A wet snow began to fall. I pulled the thin cloak more closely about me.

An old babushka with no teeth held up a picture

of the Tsar and Empress. Children waved small Russian flags, hopping from one foot to the other to keep warm. The cannons from the Peter and Paul Fortress sounded a twenty-one-gun salute. Cheers grew into a roar. The crowd pushed toward the street, carrying us with them. There, right in front of us, rolled the scarlet-and-gold carriage of the Tsar and Empress. Soldiers stationed along the curb stretched out their arms to hold the crowd back, but the people hurtled forward like a runaway train. I saw one of the soldiers aim his gun at the crowd, but an officer knocked it aside. The crowd were loyal subjects of the Tsar and asked nothing more than to get a little closer to the ruler they loved.

The crowd poured into the street to see the carriage with its team of six white horses and its gold-jacketed coachmen. It was a miracle that no one was caught beneath the carriage wheels. I looked up, and there was Tsar Nikolai in his uniform, golden epaulettes on his shoulders, rows of brightly colored decorations splashed across his chest. He looked amused rather than frightened by the crowd, but Empress Alexandra had a look of terror on her pale face. With one hand she clutched the diamond crown nestled on her red-gold hair, and with the other hand she clasped a necklace with a pink pearl as large as a sparrow's egg. From the look of fear on her face you might have thought the crowd was after her jewels. As the carriage wheeled into the entrance of the cathedral, the crowd drew back like a huge beast letting out its breath.

I was giddy with excitement. I poked Misha cruelly. "There, you see. The people love the Tsar."

Misha shrugged. "Even starving people like a good show, Katya. Now come inside before you get trampled and I get blamed. And Katya, you must promise not to tell your mama of our little adventure."

"I promise."

At the mansion I pulled off the cloak, still damp from the wet snow. There was a tear in it. "I hope no one sees me put it back," I whispered.

Misha gave me yet another of the looks that always make me feel guilty. "I didn't tear the cloak," I protested. "It happened in the crowd."

"Here. This will buy a new one." Misha slipped some rubles into the cloak's pocket. I gave him a sullen look, angry that the generous gesture had not been mine. That was another fault of Misha's. He was better than me.

I kept my promise not to tell Mama. When she returned from the cathedral, she was in a good mood. She let me sit cross-legged on her bed while she changed from her court dress with the train and the red sash across her chest to the ball gown she would wear later that evening. Breathing in her perfume and the scent of her powder was like a stroll in a garden. Her gown was white silk with tucks and pleats and a froth of lace at the neck and around the sleeves. It was so delicious, it looked like you could eat it with a spoon. Before she slipped the dress over her petticoats, I was allowed to help Mama's maid, Anya, tug the laces of Mama's corset to nip in her waist.

Tiny and birdlike, Anya hopped around like a little sparrow, a *vorobyei*. She did everything for Mama. When I was grown, I would have my own Anya to fix my hair and keep my dresses nicely and to order about as Mama ordered Anya about.

Anya hopped up on a stool to fashion Mama's golden-brown hair into twists and curls. As she worked, Mama gossiped with her about the ceremony.

"It was sad. The little Tsarevich, Alexei, was so ill, he had to be carried into the ceremony. Then such a disgraceful thing happened." Mama's face in the mirror was frowning. "That despicable creature Rasputin insisted on sitting in the section assigned to the imperial family. He had to be led out of the cathedral." Mama shuddered. "Certainly it was an inauspicious beginning for the ceremony."

I had heard about Rasputin, whom some called a holy man. Everyone knew that he was much admired by the Empress. "If he is so bad," I asked, "why does the Empress like him so much?"

Mama had forgotten I was there. When she heard my question, she gave me a sharp look, then turned back to Anya. "Anya, go and see that Vadim has the carriage ready. Katya, come and help me to fasten my sapphire necklace."

Holding the sapphires in my hands was like holding bits of the clearest, deepest blue water. I thought of how, when I was little, Mama let me take out, one by one, diamonds, emeralds, and sapphires from her jewel box to hold up to the sunlight.

As I fumbled with the necklace's clasp, Mama said, "I should not have spoken in that way about Rasputin, Katya, and you must never repeat what I said. Whatever his faults, he is a holy man, and he has been of the greatest service to the Empress in her worries over Alexei."

Alexei was the only son of the Tsar and the Empress. First there were four daughters, one after the other. Just when everyone thought there would be no heir to the throne, Alexei was born.

"Mama, what is wrong with Alexei?" He was often seen being carried about. Everyone knew that he was not well, but no one knew what the trouble was.

"He is a delicate child, that's all." After first arranging her skirts so that they would not be crushed, Mama settled next to me and took my hands in hers. Her eyes were bright and her cheeks flushed. I thought how pretty she was and despaired over ever having her beauty, for my nose was stubby rather than slender like Mama's. You could barely see my pale eyelashes, while Mama's were a thick, dark fringe.

"Katya, I wish I could wait until tomorrow when there would be more time to talk calmly with you, but I must give the Empress an answer this evening." Mama's chin was in the air, and her graceful neck was stretched out. I could tell something had happened to make her proud. She took a deep breath. "Empress Alexandra has done me a great honor, Katya. She has asked me to come to the Alexander Palace and be one of her ladies-in-waiting. And of course you would come with me."

"Oh, Mama!" The breath went out of me. I knew the Empress was fond of Mama. My governess, Lidya, had told me Mama was one of the few women at the court who understood the Empress. Many thought the Empress cold and aloof, but Mama had told me she was only shy. Empress Alexandra had come to Russia as the bride of the Tsar. She had been a princess from a small German state and could hardly speak Russian. Lidya said the glitter and sophistication of the Russian court had overwhelmed the Empress, who had drawn inside herself.

The task of the ladies-in-waiting, though it was more a privilege than a task, was to see to all the little things that made life more comfortable for the Empress. Ladies-in-waiting did her errands, answered her letters, and kept her company. I was proud of Mama's honor, but I guessed what it would mean.

"We'll have to leave our home here, won't we?" The Zhukovsky mansion had been in Mama's family since the reign of Peter the Great, over two hundred years ago.

Mama looked about the rooms as if she were considering how they might all be packed into a box. With a sigh she said, "*Da,*" and nodded. "We'll have to stay at the Alexander Palace, but we'll keep our house open for the sake of the servants, and of course Misha must continue to live here. And there will be occasions on her travels when the Empress might take another lady-in-waiting with her, and we can return home." Mama was looking closely at me. I was not sure I wanted to leave my dear home. I considered creating a fuss, insisting I didn't want to go. Perhaps Mama would make some excuse to the Empress. At the same time I was excited at the idea of living in a palace.

"What about the Grand Duchesses?" I asked. I worried that the four daughters of the Tsar and the

Empress would look down on me because I was not
royalty.

"They are another reason for our going. The
youngest, Anastasia, is eleven, only a year younger than
you. The Empress thinks the two of you would get on
well. All the girls are well behaved. They have not been
pampered. They take cold baths every morning and
have their lessons with a tutor just as you do. It will be
a great advantage for you to share those lessons."

Mama got up and shook out her skirts. "Now that
is enough, Katya. There will be plenty of time for
questions tomorrow, and we won't be going to the
Alexander Palace for a while yet. You will have plenty
of time to get used to the idea." Mama gave me a
searching look. "Shall I tell the Empress I would be
honored to be her lady-in-waiting?"

I nodded. Mama swept up her sable cape. She
reached down to give me a quick hug, and her sapphire necklace scratched my cheek. She hurried from
the room.

I tried to feel honored, but I knew that from now on our lives would depend on the plans and the whims of the Tsar and the Empress. Their wishes would be our commands. And what would the girls be like? Maybe taking a cold bath every morning would put you in a bad mood for the rest of the day.

I would have to leave my beloved St. Petersburg. The Alexander Palace was in Tsar's Village, a town twenty-six kilometers away. I thought of all I would have to give up. Just yesterday, Lidya and I had wandered into Peto's toy shop and stopped at Eliseev's Food Emporium on the Nevsky, where Lidya had read off a list Mama had given her. Later in the day Eliseev's carriage would deliver to our house baskets of delicacies: jars of caviar, plump peaches from the Crimea, and shortbread from Scotland that melted in your mouth.

After Eliseev's we had gone to my favorite place, the *perina* stalls, where Lidya rooted about in the soft feathers, discussing with the old peasant ladies from the country the quality and loft of this kind of goose down or that. In a few days' time the down we purchased would be sewed into comforters, so that I would fall asleep wrapped in clouds.

On our way home we had watched workmen cutting chunks of ice the color of Mama's aquamarine ring to store in the icehouses for summer. The city's frozen canals were slick paths for sleighs and skaters. When spring arrived, I wondered, would I be there to see the icebreakers steam down the river and hear St. Petersburg ring with the crack and tear of the ice as it gave way to the icebreakers' iron prows?

How I would miss the city when Mama became a lady-in-waiting. I tried to weigh the loss against all the new discoveries to come, but it is hard to give up what you know for what you don't know.

That evening, with Mama out, Misha and I dined alone. When there were just the two of us, the footmen served us and then left us to manage on our own.

As soon as they were out of the room, Misha began to complain. "The speech the Tsar made today is in the newspapers. The words were so cold, he must have written it in ice water. There was no promise to let the people vote, no relief from crushing taxes, no mention of a free press or an end to arresting people for speaking their thoughts."

I hardly listened to Misha's complaints, for I was waiting for a chance to tell my news. When at last he finished, I put an important look on my face and whispered to Misha, "I have a secret."

"Fine. Don't tell me, or it will no longer be a secret." Misha could be infuriating.

"I won't!" I said. "Never mind that I'm going to live in the Alexander Palace with the Tsar and the Empress."

"Impossible!" Misha dropped his knife and fork and stared at me. "What are you talking about?"

Gratified, I became busy with my cutlets.

"Katya, what do you mean?"

Smugly I said, "It's a secret. You said if I told you, it wouldn't be a secret anymore." But I was too excited to hold back. In a moment the whole story tumbled out. "And I'm to be a special friend to Grand Duchess Anastasia."

"You will not be a special friend. You will be her glorified *sluzhanka*, spending all your time bowing and scraping like a servant."

"That's not true," I said. "Mama says the Tsar's daughters are very nice girls. Lidya is friends with one of their governesses, who says they are not spoiled at all. I happen to know they take cold baths every morning, which is more than you do."

"Living in the Alexander Palace will be like living in a prison," Misha warned. "You won't be able to go anywhere without soldiers guarding you."

Irritated that Misha was trying to spoil everything, I snarled at him in French, for a footman had come into the room. "You're just jealous." I knew it infuriated Misha when people spoke French in front of servants so they could not understand. I was so angry, I wouldn't even give Misha half my dessert, something I always did, because he loved sweets so and because I wanted a waist as small as Mama's when I grew up.

Misha relented. I think he sometimes got tired of taking himself so seriously. After supper, instead of disappearing into his room with his books or going off to see friends, he played chess with me in the little parlor. The warmth from the great porcelain stove that stretched to the ceiling, the French carpet woven with roses, and the tapestries with their summer scenes of people frolicking in the woods all made winter seem far away. Because Misha was so good at chess, he usually gave me little hints and even let me take back moves. This time he was ruthless.

"You must get used to losing, Katya," he said. "At the palace the royals always win." With a grin, he added, "Since you will be such good friends with the Tsar, you must ask him when everyone can vote and when we will have freedom of speech, and when the peasants will get a decent piece of land of their own."

"The Tsar is too busy for such nonsense," I snapped.

Misha's grin disappeared. The serious look I had grown to hate came over his face. I prepared myself to be scolded, but he only kissed my forehead and sent me to bed.

"I won't spoil your dreams," he said. "Plenty of time for that. If you are a good girl, I'll take you tobogganing tomorrow on the hill across from St. Isaac's Cathedral."

That night, as I lay warm under my comforter, half listening for Mama's return from the ball, my excitement wore off. It would be a very great privilege to live in the palace, but here in the Zhukovsky mansion everything centered around me. Misha called me spoiled, but it wasn't my fault that Papa had died in a war and Mama had only me and Misha to love. As a lady-in-waiting, Mama would have to spend her days doing what the Empress wished. There would be little time left over for me. I would have to say good-bye to Lidya as well, since I would be having my lessons with Anastasia and her tutor.

And what would Anastasia be like? I did not mind the thought of playing with Anastasia and her sisters, but would I have to kneel down to them? Would I have to let them win at chess because they were the daughters of the Tsar? What if I had to take cold baths?

CHAPTER TWO

THE WINTER PALACE

Spring 1913

We learned that we were to go to the palace in September. In early May the Tsar and his family traveled south to the Crimea in search of sun and warmth. Even the Tsar of all the Russias could not warm St. Petersburg while jagged chunks of ice from the north made their way down the Neva River. In June the imperial family would go sailing on their yacht.

That spring I coaxed Lidya to go about the city with me. I was saying good-bye to my favorite places. We walked along the river and canals, watching the ferries and the barges loaded with firewood brought from the forests of Finland. Trees were scarce on the swampland on which St. Petersburg is built. After the barges were unloaded, we saw the barges themselves taken apart and made into firewood.

We spent afternoons in the Summer Garden, where army officers, along with the best of St. Petersburg society, exercised their horses. I sniffed the roses that grew there and cooled my hands under the water that tumbled from the fountains. While I wandered about, Lidya sat stiffly on a bench, holding her green parasol over her head like a small tree to protect her fair complexion from the sun.

June brought the *beliye nochi*, the white nights when it was light until two or three in the morning. Coax as I might, Lidya made me go to bed at my regular time, drawing the heavy draperies against the daylight. But there were evenings when Mama, just home from some reception or ball, would allow me to stand on the balcony of her bedroom in my nightdress.

There, long past midnight, the whole city was parading cheerfully up and down the prospekt, as if the extra hours of daylight were a lavish gift to be recklessly squandered.

While Mama and I waited for the Tsar's return, we began preparations for our new life. Madame LaMott came with her sewing machine. Madame, who was plump, looked like a porcupine with a pincushion tied to one wrist and pins bristling from her mouth. She spat out a pin or two with every word. Though Madame's taste in clothes for Mama was excellent, she herself wore dresses that looked as though they had once been piano shawls or window draperies. I was glad to see her, for she always brought me chocolates from Paris.

You could not move in the sewing room without tripping over paper patterns and snippets of ribbon and lace. Soon a trunk was filled, and then another and another.

Misha watched our preparations with disdain. He

had his own life. Mama was so taken up with packing, she didn't notice his late hours or the strange appearance of the young men who called for him. Some of them were a year older than Misha and already at the university. Their clothes were shabby, and they talked in low, conspiratorial voices, calling one another "tovarich." When I asked Misha about them, he said, "Their heads are filled with ideas, Katya, not clothes." That wasn't a nice thing to say about me, or a true one, for my head was full of ideas about how my life was going to change.

The second week in June Mama and I were to meet the Tsar and his family and to spend the night at the Winter Palace. Mama was to attend a court ball there given by the Tsar and the Empress. The Alexander Palace had only a hundred rooms, none of them suitable for a ball, while the Winter Palace had a thousand rooms spread over twenty acres. The Tsar and Empress could give as many balls there as they wished.

Strolling along the banks of the Neva River with Lidya, I had passed the Winter Palace many times. It was one of our favorite walks. When the sun shone a certain way, the reflection of the palace lay quivering on the water as if there were a second palace inhabited by mermaids. The other side of the palace overlooked a great square, and in the center of the square a granite column soared heavenward. At the top of the column, which celebrated Russia's victory over Napoleon, was a bronze angel. Lidya promised me, "Difficult times and even wars may come to the city, but as long as the angel watches over St. Petersburg, the city will survive."

I had longed to see the inside of the Winter Palace, but now that the moment had come, I cowered behind Mama. The palace entrance hall, with its white marble stairway, was three stories high. Right away I felt small. The walls were mirrored. I couldn't avoid seeing my insignificant and puny self dwarfed by all the grandeur.

In a parade of three, Mama and I followed behind a footman wearing a shako, a high hat trimmed with a feather. He led us though rooms whose walls were covered with damask and hung floor to ceiling with paintings. Overhead were crystal chandeliers that might have been carved from ice, under our feet were rugs that seemed too beautiful to step on, and everywhere was the kind of carved and gilded furniture that was torture to sit on. It was more museum than palace, and I wondered how I could sleep in such a place.

At last we came to the wing where the imperial family lived. The Empress and her children were taking tea in a room whose walls were decorated with malachite pillars. I knew how precious the green stone was, for I had a treasured ring with a tiny chip of malachite, and here was a whole room of it!

The Empress herself greeted us. I thought her very beautiful. She was tall, with a wide forehead, and an aristocratic nose. Her eyes were large and friendly, with no trace of the frightened look she had worn in the carriage. Yet I thought I glimpsed a wistful sadness, as if she were used to putting on welcoming smiles for strangers, like putting on a new dress over worn-out petticoats.

After Mama and I curtsied, and kissed her hand, the Empress put her arm around Mama. "Irina Petrovna, you are most welcome." She turned to me. "And this is dear Ekaterina Ivanova! What a charming creature, with eyes like a June sky. The girls and I are having our tea. You must join us. The Tsar will be here later. It is terrible how he is bothered by the state ministers. If only his critics knew how he sacrifices his life to the country." She shook her head angrily, as if the state ministers had no other purpose than to torment the Tsar.

Grouped around a small tea table were four girls and a boy: the Grand Duchesses and the Tsarevich, Alexei. The girls, all dressed alike, rose from their chairs in welcome, so I immediately gave up any fear

of having to kneel down before them. As I was introduced to each girl, a simple curtsy seemed all that was
required.

I had memorized the Grand Duchesses' ages.
Olga, who was eighteen, had her hair waved and
pulled back into a grown-up knot. She appeared a
little haughty and had a stubborn mouth. I could see
she wished to be treated as an adult, for she kept herself a little apart from her brother and sisters. Tatiana
was sixteen, dark-haired and, like her mother, tall and
slim with a classic beauty. Marie, fourteen, was like a
painting of an angel, with golden hair and enormous
blue eyes. Anastasia, who was eleven, was plump,
with long curls and a fringe across her forehead. She
had a mischievous look, as if she were thinking up
some devilment. Alexei, not quite nine, very pale and
with a sweet smile, did not get up. The Empress
quickly explained, "You must excuse Alexei. He has
not been well. This is his first day out of bed." There
was that sad look on her face again.

To cover the awkwardness of our first meeting, we all turned eagerly to our buttered bread and our glasses of tea, served in silver holders. I wished that Misha were there to see how simple the tea was, how there were none of the cakes and sweet biscuits we had at home for our tea. Mother and the Empress chatted away, but the girls and Alexei said little. The girls had embroidery hoops on their laps, and from time to time they would take them up and work a few stitches. After what seemed hours, but was only a few minutes, the Empress turned to Anastasia and said, "Take Ekaterina Ivanova and show her a bit of the palace, dear."

Anastasia appeared as relieved as I was to be dismissed and half walked, half skipped out of the room, while I backed awkwardly out after her, for I had been warned that it was impolite to turn your back on the Tsar or the Empress. As soon as we were out of hearing distance from the others, Anastasia asked, "What do your friends call you?"

"Katya," I said.

"Then that is what I will call you, since you are to be my *podruga*. As my close friend, you can call me Stana. Would you like to see my papa's bathroom?"

I thought that was a very strange place to begin a tour, but I was too shy to say so. In one of the rooms she paused to show me a golden Easter egg, which opened at the touch of a button to reveal a tiny train that could be wound up. "It is just like Papa's train that we take on all our trips." Stana unfastened another egg, and there was a miniature of the scarlet-and-gold carriage in which Misha and I had seen her parents riding. Scattered over the tabletops were small gold boxes set with precious stones and, best of all, tiny vases fashioned of crystal with enameled and jeweled flowers. *"Krasivo,"* I said, sighing, for it was very beautiful. I would have been content to stay and examine such treasures, but Stana pulled me along.

I held my breath as we entered what must have been the imperial bedroom. I was so awed at being in the room that I crossed it on tiptoe, trying to keep out of my head any disrespectful pictures of the Tsar and Empress in their nightshirts. The room was covered with lilac-and-white striped silk. Garlands of flowers were painted on the ceiling, and the walls were hung with portraits of Alexei and his sisters and with hundreds of icons, paintings of Jesus or Mary or the saints. I felt like all of heaven was looking down on me and frowning at my trespass.

Stana opened a door with a flourish, and there was not just a bathroom but a kind of swimming pool. A swimming pool inside a house! I had never heard of such a thing. The floor of the room was white marble. The pool itself was a kind of tank with a marble bottom.

Stana closed the door behind us. "Let's go for a swim," she said, "only we mustn't get our hair wet or they'll know." Stana was already slipping out of her dress and petticoats. I was sure I shouldn't follow her example, but I was tempted, for I had never gone swimming inside a house before. The next thing I knew, I was shedding my own petticoats.

No one but Lidya and Mama had seen me without clothes, but Stana seemed to think nothing of slipping naked into the pool. In a moment we were splashing around in water warm as soup. The walls of the room were hung with paintings of seascapes and naval battles, so I imagined that I was swimming in an ocean.

We both tried very hard to keep our heads out of the water, but a few minutes later, when we climbed out of the pool and into our clothes, I was alarmed to find we both had wet curls!

On the way back Stana and I wandered up and down stairs, and from one wing of the palace to another, taking our time in the hopes that our hair would dry. In one hallway we found two footmen, felt pads on their feet, skating back and forth, buffing a wooden floor.

When we reached the kitchens, I saw what appeared to be half a cow, roasting on a spit. Stana dipped her finger into a bowl of custard and licked her finger, then coaxed two pieces of cake from one of the cooks. "Come, Toma, we are starving. The bread at tea was sliced so thin, you could see through it, and there was no jam."

Toma, a stout woman with kind eyes and hair tied back in a kerchief, must have been used to such pleadings, for she laughed and handed us each a large slice of butter cake. "Here, then, but no word to the Empress or there will be trouble for both of us." I thought it odd that the daughter of the Tsar should have to beg for food.

After we left the kitchens, we entered a billiard room, where Stana picked up a cue and, with an expert poke, shot a ball across the table. As we passed a closed door, she said, "This is Papa's office, where all day long he signs important papers. One day, if he lives, my brother, Alexei, will be Tsar and sign papers in there."

"If he lives? What's wrong with your brother?"

Stana gave me a quick look. "We're not supposed to say, but since you're to be my *podruga*, I'll tell you if you promise not to tell anyone else. The Russian people mustn't find out the heir to the throne is very sick."

I promised to say nothing.

"My brother has hemophilia. If he suffers the least little bump or fall, he begins to bleed, and the bleeding won't stop. Sometimes the bleeding is inside of Alexei's body, and then he is in pain, which makes poor Mama cry. Mama blames herself, because the hemophilia was inherited from her grandmother Queen Victoria's family. Mama's little brother, Frittie, had it, and he died when he was only three, so she worries about Alexei all the time."

I was shocked. I could not imagine the tall regal Empress crying. "Can't the doctors do something for Alexei?"

"*Nyet*." She shook her head. "There is no medicine. The doctors can't do anything. Only Rasputin can help him."

"Rasputin?" I remembered Mama's disgust when she mentioned his name.

Stana nodded. "Yes, the holy peasant. Mama and Papa call him Father Grigory, but he is nothing like a priest. When he fixes his eyes on Alexei, and speaks to him in a soothing voice, Alexei gets better. I don't like Rasputin. He is like a dog we once had that groveled when Papa or Mama was there but bit you when no one was looking. Worse, Rasputin smells like a barnyard. Now we had better go back, or Mama will send someone after us."

We found the Tsar sitting between the Empress and Mama, chatting away, a glass of tea in his hand. I could hardly believe this slight man with gentle blue eyes and a soft mouth, nearly hidden in his silky brown beard and mustache, was Nikolai II. I remembered seeing him in his scarlet-and-gold coach, and once I had stood with Mama and seen him mounted on a horse reviewing his troops. The soldiers had fallen on their knees before him. He had looked much larger then.

The Tsar smiled at me. "So, you are to be the companion to my little Stana. We are very pleased to have you." He reached over and patted Stana's damp curls and then mine. He gave us a knowing look, and with horror I saw that he guessed we had been splashing in his bath. There was no scolding. He only smiled and said, "I hope, Katya, that you will be a good influence on Stana. She does not always think before she acts."

I had been in the palace for only a few hours, and already I had let down the Tsar of all the Russias. I was mortified, and I resolved I would not let Stana talk me into more mischief.

The Tsar turned back to Mama and the Empress and went on with his conversation. Now his words were no longer gentle, as they had been to us. "There will always be people out there who dare to question the authority of the Tsar," he said in a stern voice. "I let the people have a parliament and even let it meet in my own palace. What is my reward? The members of that Duma begin to tell me how to run my country—

me, the Tsar. My grandfather freed the serfs, and what were his thanks? They murdered him! This is an autocracy and always will be. It is not some mindless democracy where the people act like spoiled children and do just as they please. In such countries the people vote for those who shout the loudest and promise them the most. I mean to strike down with a firm hand anyone who attacks the empire."

At these words I trembled for Misha. What if someone had overheard him criticizing the Tsar? I did not want Misha to be struck down with a firm hand.

"It is only in the cities like St. Petersburg and Moscow that these dangerous revolutionaries are found," the Empress said to the Tsar. "In the countryside, which is the real Russia, the peasants all love you and would willingly give their lives for you."

"*Da, da,*" Mama agreed. "At my dacha, The Oaks, all those on my small estate think of the Tsar as a god."

The Empress looked pleased. "There, you see, my dear," she said. "What did I tell you?"

The Tsar patted the Empress's hand. "Yes, I know you are right, my dear. Now I must excuse myself. There is always work to be done."

Shortly after the Tsar left, Mama and I were shown to our rooms in another wing of the palace. As we looked about at our pretty quarters, Mama warned me, "Enjoy this luxury while you can, Katya. I have heard the Alexander Palace is more plain."

"The tea was very plain, Mama."

"Yes, Katya. The Tsar and the Empress have no wish to make a show of their wealth. What's more, they are determined to bring up the Grand Duchesses in as simple a way as possible. They don't want their children to be spoiled or arrogant."

My own life at the Zhukovsky mansion was not so simple. I wondered if Misha was right, and I really was spoiled.

That evening I sighed as I watched Mama dress for the ball. I would have given anything to see such a spectacle. "Be patient, Katya. One of these days you will be the belle of the ball."

"One of these days" seemed a lifetime away. After Mama left, I sat at her dressing table and stared into the mirror. A child stared back at me. I tried pinning up my hair, but I was clumsy and only managed to look like those birds with a topknot that sticks up. I daubed on some of Mama's Coty perfume and wound one of her sable scarfs around my neck. I was just about to slide on an elbow-length kidskin glove when there was a knock at the door. Hastily I snatched off the fur and let down my hair. I opened the door to Stana.

She looked conspiratorially about her and then slid into the room. "Do you want to see the ball?" she asked. "I know a place where we can watch and no one can see us."

I forgot all about the Tsar's request that I set a good example for Stana. "*Khorosho*," I eagerly agreed. I followed Stana down the hall. Then began a journey through the palace. Where a room was empty, we ran. Where there were servants about, we walked purposefully, as if we had been sent on an errand. Finally Stana led me through a door and up several flights of dark, narrow stairs, until at last she opened a small door that led to a narrow balcony. I could hear music and the sound of voices. She motioned me to come close to the edge.

There below us was a ballroom filled with hundreds of swirling couples. Most of the men were in uniform—some in white jackets, some in red, and some in blue. The jackets were covered with gold trim, and there were red sashes across the men's chests, and rows of decorations. The men were more colorful than the women, but the women in their light silks seemed to float over the dance floor. In an enclosure topped with a red-velvet canopy sat the Empress and the ladies-in-waiting, Mama among them. Standing behind them were the Tsar and the Grand Dukes, all with the blue sash of the court across their chests.

Stana pointed out one of the Grand Dukes.

"That's my uncle," she said. "Papa is very angry with him, because he wants to marry a ballerina. That would be a great shame for our family. In front of him is my grandmama Marie. She gave a ball in her St. Petersburg palace for Olga and Tatiana. They danced until four in the morning, and the orchestra played tangos! Mama won't let them go there again unless she's with them. Over there—the woman with the pink dress and the red hair—she had to sell her jewels because her husband gambles at cards."

Stana had many such stories, but I didn't listen. With the dancers swirling below me and the waltzes drifting upward, I didn't want unpleasant stories in my head. I wanted only to look and look so that what I was seeing would stay in my memory forever.

CHAPTER THREE

MISHA'S ST. PETERSBURG

Summer 1913

I could not wait to return home and fill Misha's ears with the wonders I had seen at the palace. Misha spoiled my stories by scolding, "Thousands of rubles for such extravagance while half the city goes to bed hungry."

"But Misha, the Tsar and his family have nothing but buttered bread for tea, no cakes or sweets."

"And footmen to serve it and a silver samovar," Misha mocked.

"We have footmen here, and why should you be against pretty things?"

"I know we have footmen here; it's a great embarrassment to me. And I'm not against pretty things. But
why should one person have them and not another?
You don't want to believe it, Katya, but I promise you
a revolution is coming. In the Black Sea a part of the
Russian navy has mutinied."

I shrugged. "The Black Sea is far away."

"You don't even know what goes on right here
under your nose in St. Petersburg."

"That's not true! Lidya and I walk everywhere in
the city."

"There are places Lidya doesn't take you."

"Then take me yourself," I challenged him.
"Tomorrow Lidya leaves to visit her sister in Moscow,
and Mama is going to a reception."

He shook his head. "Such places are not for you.
They would only make you unhappy."

I teased him until he finally agreed. "Very well, but
don't blame me if you don't like what you see. And,
Katya"—he frowned at my dress with its sash and silk

ruffles—"dress in the simplest clothes you have. I don't want people staring at us."

The next morning, as soon as Mama and Lidya left, I changed into a plain white blouse, a dark skirt, and a straw hat I had once sat upon. I hurried downstairs, eager for my adventure. Misha was there, but I could see from the unwelcoming expression on his face that he regretted his invitation.

Once outside he strode rapidly along the Nevsky as if he hoped I would tire and drop away. All of St. Petersburg was suffering with the heat. Dampness crept up from the river and canals and oozed down from the gray clouds that clotted the sky and threatened rain. As I hurried after Misha, I felt that with every step I was parting thick, muggy air.

As we passed the city's library, Misha was careful to keep his distance from me. He often met his friends there and would not want to be seen with some young girl tagging after him. The library faced a large square with a monument to Ekaterina the Great. It was the

Empress Ekaterina that I was named after. Though she was called "the Great," she was not an especially nice ruler, what with murdering her husband and taking a lover who was such a peacock that he had millions of rubles worth of diamonds sewn on his suit.

A little farther along the Nevsky we came to my favorite bridge, the Anichkov, with its great prancing bronze horses. We crossed the Fontanka Canal and walked by Moscow Station, where all day long trains arrived and left on their journeys to Moscow. It was where Mama and I took the train when we journeyed to The Oaks. We passed the station, leaving the center of the city that I knew, with its fine homes and elegant shops now behind us.

Misha turned down a narrow street and slowed to my pace, taking hold of my arm. People were staring at us, for we clearly did not look like we belonged there. The homes were simple wooden buildings with a few goats or a pig in each yard. I wanted to hang over the fences and pat the goats, with their floppy ears and yellow eyes, but Misha pulled me along.

There were dreary-looking factories set among the homes. Misha turned into one of them. As he opened the door and pushed me through, I was overcome with the heat and stench. I held my nose. "Ugh, what is it?" I whispered.

We were in a large, cavernous room crowded with people picking through bins of soiled rags. More rags were heaped in baskets and tied in bales. "What are they doing?"

"They're sorting the rags, which are used to make paper," Misha said.

"But the rags are filthy. How can they touch them? Won't the paper be dirty?"

"People don't throw away clean rags. Before they are made into paper, they will be boiled in lye."

I was amazed to see that most of the workers were boys and girls, some of them younger than I was. They were all dressed alike, the boys in peasant smocks and trousers, the girls in plain dresses, their hair covered with kerchiefs. "Why are there so many children?" I asked.

"Their wages are low. They'll work all day for next to nothing."

"And when school starts again?"

"This is their school. This is what they learn."

"Surely the government should be told. They would not allow such a thing."

"It's the Tsar's government that employs them, Katya. These dirty rags will be turned into government paper to do the government's dirty business."

I started to protest, but I couldn't find the words. By now some of the children had noticed us and paused in their work to stare. One of them was a girl who looked my age. Her face was pinched and thin, and she had enormous brown eyes with dark circles under them. A skimpy braid hung down her back. She was looking so hard at me that I started to walk toward her, thinking to speak to her, but two inspectors noticed us. They shouted at the children to get back to work and headed in our direction. Quickly Misha pulled me out into the street. As hot as it was, it was ten times cooler than it had been inside, and I dared to breathe again.

"For once, Katya, you have nothing to say."

I didn't. I was thinking what it would be like to awaken in the morning, knowing you would spend all day in such a place, and worse still, the next day and the day after.

"Why don't they complain?" I asked.

Misha shrugged. "They need the work in order to eat. Anyhow, who would listen to them? They are only children. Now I'll show you some workers who do complain."

While I followed Misha, a plan was forming in my mind. I did not care what Misha said about the Tsar's government being the one that employed the children in such miserable work. I was sure that if he knew of it, the Tsar would never allow such a thing. His government must be keeping it a secret from him. The gentle man who sat nibbling on the bit of buttered bread, the kindly man who patted Stana's and my wet curls with no scolding, would put an end to such a horror. I resolved to find a way to tell the Tsar.

Thinking only of my plan, I trotted along after Misha through streets and alleys until we came to a square wooden building. A group of women were carrying placards on sticks. They walked back and forth, holding up their signs. At first I thought they were some sort of street amusement, like the man with the dancing bear Lidya and I often saw on the palace square, or the Gypsies with their tambourines who danced to invite coins.

Yet these women had no costume, and there was no music or dance, only a kind of sad marching back and forth. As we got closer, I could read the signs. WE DEMAND A FIFTY-FIVE-HOUR WEEK, one said. On another was written: A FAIR WAGE.

The woman who was leading the march was about my mama's age, but stocky with fat red cheeks and a tangle of black hair that had not seen a comb for some time. The hardness in her eyes told me that the marching was not an entertainment but something much more serious. Misha clapped her on the shoulder as one man would another. "Galya, tovarich, how goes it?" he asked.

"My little Misha, have you come to give us a hand? Where are the other students? All asleep in their comfy beds, the lazy fellows. They promised they would be here this morning. I should have known better. You aristocrats are all alike. You encourage us to strike, but you are never here when we need you."

So that was what it was. A *zabastovka*. I had heard Mama complain when some shoes she had ordered did not arrive because the factory was on strike. "Why should there be a strike?" she had asked. "The workmen are lucky to have a job." Angrily she had decided to buy shoes from another factory. She had vowed, "Never again will those men get my trade."

Recalling Mama's words, I said to Galya, "But you all have jobs."

She looked at me as if she would have liked to put out her hand and brush me away like a troublesome fly. Turning to Misha, she said, "What is this? You have brought me a little aristocrat who has never done a day's work in her life to stand here and sneer at me." Then she laughed. "Never mind. It's time we understood that we are on our own with no one we can depend upon. You revolutionaries come to our meetings and encourage us to strike. You say, 'It is only right that you should demand enough money to eat.' Where are you brave revolutionaries now? All you want is trouble for the Tsar, so you can have the country to play with like some spoiled child who sees a toy he must have."

For once Misha was without words. Finally he managed to say, "That's unfair, Galya. We do support you. We won't let you down. You can count on us joining in the demonstration."

Just then four Cossacks, special guards on horse-back, rounded the corner. The women stopped marching and stared at them. One of the Cossacks shouted, "This *zabastovka* is illegal. Disperse at once!" He had a whip, which he raised as his horse cantered toward the women.

Terrified, the women huddled about Galya as if they were chicks seeking shelter beneath the wings of a mother hen. Galya did not move but stood glaring at the policemen.

Misha grabbed me by the arm, and we began to run. When we were at a safe distance, I glanced back. The Cossacks were lashing at the fleeing women with their whips. I stopped running and began to wail. Misha put his hand over my mouth and dragged me away.

When we had put several blocks between us and the women, Misha paused so that we could catch our breath. I asked, "Why did you run away?"

Misha's face became white. I saw that my question

infuriated him. "Because I had you with me. Was I to leave you to be trampled by those horses?"

"You could have told me to run. If you had stayed, the Cossacks might have listened to you."

"They listen to no one. And you are not the one to tell me what I must do. You are a useless, spoiled child, a lapdog to amuse the Tsar's daughters. You'll fritter away your days in a palace while the citizens of St. Petersburg plan to tear the palace down. You're no better than one of the Tsar's fifteen thousand servants."

I was indignant. "The people love the Tsar, and he loves them. How can he know everything that goes on in the city? When I tell him about the children and the rags, he will put a stop to it. You wait and see."

We were back on the Nevsky Prospekt. People were staring at us. We fell silent, walking the rest of the way home without a word. The sun had broken through the clouds, and the day was hotter than ever. My blouse clung damply to my arms and chest. I was grateful to escape into our cool, high-ceilinged mansion.

Once we were inside, Misha stomped up the stairs to his room. I trailed up the stairway behind him, wandering through Mama's bedroom and into her sitting room. The sitting room, with its pale-yellow walls decorated with a border of painted flowers, was my favorite room. The windows opened out onto a balcony that overlooked the Nevsky Prospekt. Now the windows were closed against the muggy June day, and the yellow draperies were drawn. The sun filtering through the silk turned the room to gold. I could smell Mama's perfume, a fragrance like gardenias that lingered after her.

I knew I would never have the courage to tell the Tsar my story to his face, yet he had to know. In front of me was Mama's little French desk. On the desk was a neat stack of Mama's thick ivory writing paper with the family crest and her name, Countess Irina Petrovna Baronova. I wondered who had gathered the rags to make the paper.

After a moment I sat down at the desk and took up a pen. I was the one writing the letter, not Mama, so I crossed out her name. Three sheets were wasted before the letter was finished.

June 30, 1913
To Nikolai II, Tsar of all the Russias

Your very great Excellency:
With respect I would like to draw your attention to the place where they collect rags to make paper for the government. I was recently a visitor there and can tell you some things about it that I am sure you would wish to know.

First of all, the place was very hot and smelly. I, personally, could hardly breathe. The other thing is that the people who were sorting the rags, which were very dirty, were not people at all, but children. I am sure you would not want young children to work from morning to night in such a smelly place doing

such dirty work when if it weren't summer,
they should have been going to school, which
they don't even do when there is school.

Also, there are some evil Cossacks who
carry whips, which they use against helpless
women.

Russia is a very big place, so you must
have a great deal on your mind, and I know
you can't see everything that goes on. I hope
you won't mind my telling you about this, so
that you can do something to make it better.

Your devoted and humble subject,
Ekaterina Ivanova Baronova

I was concentrating so hard on writing the letter, I
didn't hear Mama come into the room. It was only
when the fragrance of perfume grew stronger that I
looked up to see her.

"Katya, what are you up to?" she asked. "Surely

you have no schoolwork in the middle of the summer?"

"I'm writing to the Tsar, Mama," I said, pride in my voice, for not everyone writes to the Tsar.

"To thank him for his hospitality at the Winter Palace? You are a good girl, Katya, but such a note should go to the Empress."

"No, something more important, Mama." Without thinking, and proud of my efforts, I held out the letter.

Mama read it over twice. First she had a puzzled look on her face and then a frightened one. "Katya, you can't send such a letter. It's impossible!"

While I watched, stunned, she tore up the letter. I felt my lips tremble, and I burst into tears. Mama tried to gather me up and comfort me, but I pushed her away.

"Katya, darling, listen to me. The Tsar has millions of subjects. He cannot concern himself with such trifles. He must attend to the important things."

"It isn't a trifle!" Suddenly Mama's fragrance, which always seemed so delicious, made me angry. "How would you like to work all day in a place that stinks?"

"Don't speak to me like that, Katya! And never use the word 'stink.' This is all Misha's doing. That boy does nothing but stir up trouble. It's that school he goes to. It's far too liberal. I'm going to speak to Grand Duke Nikolai Nikolayevich at once. He must find a place for Misha in the military academy, where the boy will be too busy to get into such mischief. I should have done it long since. I'm sure it would be what his papa would have wished. It was very bad of Misha to involve you in his treasonous affairs. If he keeps on, he will bring trouble down on all of us."

I was miserable. Not only had I gotten Misha into trouble, but Mama had said the Tsar was too busy for such things. If the Tsar was our little father, why wouldn't he want to know about the children? But Mama said he must not be bothered. It made no sense.

As soon as I could get Misha alone, I confessed in a miserable voice what had happened. "I promise I didn't tell that it was you who took me to see the rag factory. Mama guessed when she saw the letter to the Tsar."

"Your mother is smarter than you are, Katya. She knows the Tsar would not want to see a letter that tells the truth. The Tsar prefers to close his eyes to such matters."

In a shaky voice I warned him, "Misha, Mama wants you to go to the military academy and become an officer in the Tsar's army."

"I'll never do it," Misha said. His face was red with anger. "They can't make me."

"She's going to ask Grand Duke Nikolai to find a place for you."

Misha's face fell. Grand Duke Nikolai, a cousin of the Tsar, was known for his love of the army. He was six feet, six inches tall with piercing blue eyes, eagle eyes that looked right through you. The soldiers all worshiped him. "I'll run away first," Misha said, but there was less certainty in his voice. He knew he couldn't oppose the Grand Duke.

Misha stormed through the house the rest of the day, slamming doors and growling at me. After dinner, during which he hardly spoke a word, Mama took him into the parlor. They were there a long time. When he came out, he was grumbling, but there was no more talk of his running away.

He flopped down on a chair and glared at me. "They can put me in the army, but they won't silence me. Let them teach me to shoot guns. They will be sorry one day when I use them for the revolution!"

"Misha! What a terrible thing to say. You'll surely regret such words." I rushed out of the room, no longer feeling guilty for my part in what was to happen to Misha. I thought the army would be a good thing for him. I hoped they would make him march all day until he was too tired to have such thoughts.

Still, the next week, when Misha, his face stern

and pale, went off to officers' school, I threw my arms around him and began to cry.

He tried to smile. "Katya, let go of me. You are like a limpet. How can I turn into a brave soldier if I am sent off with all this weeping?"

After he left, I wailed to Mama, "He'll be killed in a war like my papa and his papa were."

"Nonsense," Mama said, trying to comfort me. "There are no wars for soldiers to fight these days. Countries are too sensible for such things."

CHAPTER FOUR

THE OAKS

Summer 1913

Mama and I always spent my August birthday at The Oaks. Misha usually went with us, but now he was at the military academy. The estate, a few hours by train and carriage from St. Petersburg, was inherited, like our mansion, from Mama's papa. At The Oaks you left the busyness of the city for a world where there seemed to be no clocks. Mama had even forbidden electricity at the dacha, so we were in a different time as well as a different world.

Vitya, the estate manager, and two coachmen met

our train in a carriage pulled by four gray horses. There was a second, smaller carriage for Lidya and Anya. Vitya was a big man, packed into his suit as tightly as a sausage into its skin. He hastened to kiss Mama's hands and to pat me on the head, saying, as he always did, "Our little flower is growing as fast as a weed." With an air of great importance he ordered the coachmen to load our trunks on the carriage, and in a minute we were galloping over the country road, Lidya and Anya behind us, hanging on to their hats.

Though Mama received a letter each month from Vitya giving an account of crops and earnings, there was still a year's worth of gossip for Vitya to tell. While Mama and Vitya chatted, I looked for the landmarks that told me we were nearing The Oaks: a narrow plank bridge that rattled in a frightening way as the carriage rolled over it; an orchard whose trees were festooned with green apples; a peasant's cottage where a flock of hissing geese attacked the carriage; and at last the double row of ancient oaks like sentinels, marching along our driveway.

The Oaks was not one of the great estates, with thousands of acres of farmland and thousands of peasants to work it. There were only eight hundred acres and a few hundred peasants. We had no showy mansion with pillars, great stairways, marble halls, and a fine park. The dacha was much more cozy. It was a long wooden building, painted green so that it blended pleasantly into the grass and trees. A wide porch ran across the front of the house. The windows were all doors, so from any room you had only to open the window and step outside, which made the inside and the outside nearly one. In the garden were endless flower beds, tables and chairs for picnics, and a croquet court of velvet grass where Misha and I battled one another. Beyond the gardens was a small orchard of cherry and apple trees, and beyond the orchard, as far as you could see, fields of oats and wheat. It was those fields that brought in money to help pay for the upkeep of our St. Petersburg mansion.

As we pulled through the carriageway and entered the courtyard, Grishka, Vitya's wife, who always saved up some small thing to complain to Mama about, hurried to greet us. She curtsied to Mama and gave me a quick nod before she began: "Madame, you are just here, so I won't trouble you at once, but there is such a problem with one of the housemaids. It is terrible how disrespectful the young have become."

She would have gone on, but Mama stopped her. "*Da, da,* Grishka. We will talk later of that. Now Katya and I are tired from our trip, and want nothing more than our tea."

At once Grishka was all business, shouting to the footmen to be careful with our luggage and summoning a maid to prepare the tea. While Lidya and Anya unpacked our trunks, Mama and I changed out of our traveling clothes into summer dresses. We settled on the porch while a young maid I had not seen before brought us a silver tray of tea and cakes with little pots of jam.

"What is your name?" Mama asked the maid, who looked eighteen or nineteen. She was very pretty, with pink cheeks, green cat's eyes, and blond braids pinned around her head like a crown.

The maid was so overcome at having a question directed at her that she was speechless for a moment. Finally, with a deep curtsy, she whispered, "Nina Yankova, Madame," and fled.

As she was leaving, Grishka appeared. She frowned as she watched the girl hurry into the house.

"I'm having trouble with that one," she told Mama.

"She seems such a sweet girl," Mama said.

"The young people are all the same these days." Grishka frowned a terrible frown and lowered her voice. "That girl wants to marry one of the field hands. We cannot have it. We must keep up the standards of the household help. After all we have done to train her to be polite and respectable, we can't have her living in a hut with a mud floor. I have forbidden the marriage."

Mama was always a little intimidated by Grishka. Besides, she hated to be in the middle of disputes between Grishka and the servants. "Well, well, Grishka, you must do as you think best. Let us talk of pleasanter things. Have you put up some of those delicious preserves for us?" My mouth watered as I thought of the barrels and boxes that arrived in St. Petersburg every fall from The Oaks.

Grishka liked nothing better than to show off her efficiency. "I had the kitchen prepare a hundred jars of wild strawberry jam, a hundred raspberry, a hundred cherry; and the blackberry and apple jellies are still to come. The pickles and sauerkraut will be ready in the fall."

I knew that soon Grishka would be telling Mama all the housekeeping problems in great detail. I stuffed another cake into my mouth and begged to be excused. A moment later I was running to the barns. I admired the cows' long eyelashes, buried my hands in the sheep's soft wool, and dirtied my dress by snatching up a piglet that had been rolling in mud. From a safe distance I looked at the workhorses with their muscled shoulders and sturdy legs. Next to the horses' stable was the smithy. The blacksmith, a cheerful, red-haired man who kept his teeth on a shelf nearby, greeted me as he always had by making me an iron ring from a nail. "There you are, Katya Ivanova. It will have to do until your sweetheart gives you a ring with a diamond."

In the fields the peasants were at work with their sickles, harvesting the grain. In the sweltering heat the men had taken off their tunics and the women worked with rolled-up sleeves. There were children in the fields not much older than me. It was late afternoon. I knew the peasants started work early in the day, for in other years I had been awakened at dawn by their voices as they started for the fields. Their calls had meant no more to me than the early calls of the doves, and I had turned over in my soft bed and gone back to sleep.

A few of the peasants stopped to look at me. In the past they would have given me friendly waves and calls of greeting, but today they only turned silently back to their work. I was hurt, but the afternoon was hot and they had been there many hours, so I thought little of it.

I had grown warm. The underarms of my dress were wet, and I felt beads of perspiration on my forehead and the back of my neck. I made my way to a small stream almost hidden in cattails and tall grasses, pulled off my shoes and stockings, and, hiking up my skirts, stepped into the cold water. The mud from the bottom of the stream oozed up between my toes. A dappled green-and-brown frog gave a great leap and disappeared into the water. Ruby-and-emerald dragonflies wove a tapestry among the grasses.

Farther upstream were deep holes where Misha and I used to fish for trout. Misha looked down on me because I used worms for bait, while he insisted on little "bugs" he made himself from bits of feather and fur. But much to his disgust, I was the one who caught the most fish. I never knew quite how to feel about Misha. Sometimes he was a brother, sometimes a friend, sometimes a tease and a vexation. Today I decided that the dacha was not as much fun without Misha.

Lidya searched me out in the grasses. "Katya! We have looked everywhere for you. Your dress is all muddy, and your hem is wet. Come and change at once. Baron Nogin is coming to dinner."

Baron Ossip Maksimovich Nogin was a widower who lived nearby on an estate much larger and grander than ours. He was older than Mama. He had a shiny bald head and was so heavy, he would have filled two chairs had it not been impolite to offer them to him. Mama always winced when he settled down on one of her elegant settees, quickly saying, "Come, that is too uncomfortable; try this." She would guide him to a sturdy overstuffed chair that I could see he hated, for he had a hard time pulling himself out of it.

Our neighbor had once been a lawyer in St. Petersburg, taking the cases of people who were too poor to hire their own lawyers. On one state occasion he had shocked everyone by refusing to drink to the Tsar's health. He wrote articles criticizing the Tsar's government and calling for a constitution. For his defiance he had been sent to jail for two months. Now he lived in a kind of exile on his estate, still writing his articles. In past years Misha had spent long hours at the baron's estate, talking with him about his ideas.

I looked forward to Baron Nogin's visits, because he always came with a present for me. That evening he handed me a cage. "There you are, Katya, a little friend."

Peeking inside the cage, I found a rabbit with such long hair, I could not tell its front from its back. At once I opened the cage and gathered its soft silkiness into my arms.

"It's an Angora rabbit," he said. "Something different. I like to try new things on my estate." He turned to Mama. "The trouble with you, Irina Petrovna, is that you leave everything to Vitya. He doesn't rotate the fields properly, and he has the peasants beaten. You won't get any work out of them that way. You should give up all that fancy living in St. Petersburg. It's a bunch of nonsense. Move down here and marry me. That's the thing to do. I'll soon get this estate in shape."

It was what Baron Nogin said each time he came. Mama laughed. "I am only a woman, Ossip. I put all those things out of my head. Vitya sends me my money, and that is all I care about."

The Baron shook his finger playfully at her. "Saying that you are only a woman, Irina Petrovna, is an excuse. It won't do. These are troubling times. In my father's day our peasants were serfs, slaves, to be bought and sold. A cruel master could do away with a troublesome serf. Those days are past, but still the peasants are overworked, with no schools for their children and without enough land to make a living.

There are men who are talking with the peasants and turning them against their masters. Estates have been pillaged and burned and their owners killed."

Mama turned away. "I don't want to hear such horror stories, Ossip Maksimovich. You are only trying to frighten me."

In a more gentle voice Baron Nogin said, "You are right. It is just what I am trying to do. You ought to realize how much your peasants hate Vitya."

Mama shrugged her shoulders and said, "Very well, I'll speak to him, but he doesn't like me to interfere. Now come and have supper, and let's talk of more pleasant things."

The Baron willingly followed Mama into the dining room, a smile on his face, for he was never more happy than when he sat down to a meal.

After Baron Nogin left, I took my rabbit outside so it could nibble on the grass. Though it was after nine o'clock, it was still light, that light that is not daytime but some extra thing saved just for summer evenings. Flowers, the night beauties and teardrops, glowed in the twilight. A nightingale trilled from a linden tree. The August air was heavy, and the windows of the sitting room were open to tempt whatever breezes there were. I heard Mama summon Vitya. As he entered the room, I could picture him bowing and scraping, as he always did in front of Mama.

"Vitya," Mama said, trying to sound masterful, "what is this I hear about you beating our peasants? I won't have that, you know."

"Oh, Madame, forgive me for saying so, but you have been listening to Baron Nogin. He makes trouble for all of us. His estate is like a kindergarten. All his peasants run about doing as they like. If I managed The Oaks like that, Madame, we should soon be in the poorhouse."

I knew that was a threat Mama hated to hear, for her expenses in St. Petersburg were large. Each month she sat at her little desk, frowning over the accounts. There were wages to be paid for my governess, my drawing master, Madame LaMott, our steward and butler, the footmen and maids, the silver polisher and cooks and laundresses, the gardeners and stable boys and coachmen. "Very well, Vitya, I leave it to you, but you must be fair with the peasants." In a weak voice she added, "I insist on that."

As I lay in bed that night, I could not get Baron Nogin's words out of my head. If what the Baron said was true, then surely Mama should help the peasants. She was so gentle and kind; how could she put up with Vitya's cruelty? Perhaps she thought the Baron was exaggerating. I remembered the stony looks I had received from the peasants. I decided the next day I would talk with one of the peasants and find out for myself if Vitya beat them. At last, as the candle at my bedside guttered out, I fell asleep to the fiddling of crickets and the rustling of the aspen leaves outside my window.

The next morning Mama was busy going over the linen supply with Grishka, who had come to her at breakfast to complain that the sheets needed mending and the tablecloths were stained.

I wandered outside to see how my rabbit was. I cuddled it for a bit, let it run about, and tore up grass to feed it. After a while I thought of my decision to talk with one of the peasants and, after putting the rabbit back in its cage, headed for the threshing barn. The barn was heaped with grain. Men stripped to the waist and women wearing kerchiefs to keep the dust from their hair were working away with flails, separating the grain from the chaff. They paid no attention to me, and after a bit I left, unsure of how to approach them.

I went into the kitchen garden to split open pea pods and eat the fresh green peas. They crunched as I bit into them, and tasted of summer. The kitchen door opened, and I saw a sobbing Nina collapse on the porch steps, her knees drawn up, her head buried in her arms. I was sure she hadn't seen me, and at first I thought I would tiptoe away. But she appeared so miserable, I asked softly, so as not to frighten her, "Nina, what's the matter?"

She began to cry harder than ever. "Vitya is sending Stepan away to the army to keep him from marrying me. They won't even let me say good-bye to him."

"But you are both of age," I said. I was filled with romantic thoughts. "Can't you run off together?"

"Oh, Miss. How should we live? We don't have a ruble in the world. If we go to another estate to ask for work, they will demand references, and where would we get them? Worse than that, they have already given Stepan's name to the army recruiter. Every village has to give so many men to the army. Now Stepan will be one of them. He will have to go into the army for years and years. If he doesn't, he will be shot as a deserter."

"Can't he get out of it?"

"Only by bribing the recruiting officer."

"How much would that take?" I asked. "I have a little money." I thought of the five rubles I had saved from my Easter gifts.

"Fifty rubles," Nina said.

I shook my head.

"Oh, Miss." Nina took my hand. "I can tell you have a kind heart. There is something you can do. Could you give Stepan this message? Tell him I will never stop loving him, however long he is gone." Hurriedly she gave me directions to Stepan's cottage. "You must go after supper. He will be in the fields now."

At that moment Grishka poked her head out of the kitchen doorway and called to Nina in a shrill voice, "What are you doing out there? Are you filling that child's head with nonsense? Come in here at once." Nina gave me a desperate look and went inside.

As soon as supper was over, I set off for Stepan's cottage. It was a long way from our house. A faint breeze ruffled the leaves at the tops of the trees, but at ground level the air was still. A ballet of swallowtail butterflies pirouetted around a honeysuckle bush. I stopped to pluck some of the blossoms and suck their sweet sap.

When I reached the small cottage with its thatched roof, I saw an old woman in the yard, sitting on a wooden stool. She was talking to herself, but every few moments she would fling her apron over her head and moan.

"Ma'am," I said, "I'm looking for Stepan."

She clapped her hands. "No, no. He has suffered enough. Please go away and leave us in peace."

I assured her that I was a friend and only wanted to deliver a message to Stepan. She flung the apron back over her head, as if she wished to hide from the world. At the sound of her cries, a young man came to the door. He had a ruddy complexion and a thatch of black hair that fell over his forehead.

He stared coldly at me. "What do you want?"

"Are you Stepan? If you are, I have a message for you from Nina."

I repeated Nina's words. Tears came to his eyes.

Angrily he brushed them away. He looked at me with disgust. "Did Vitya put you up to this so he could have me beaten again?"

Indignant, I said, "No. Truly. I saw Nina in the kitchen garden." After a moment I asked in a timid voice, "Did Vitya really have you beaten?"

For an answer he pulled off his tunic. His back was crosshatched with bloody stripes. I covered my eyes. "Why did he do it?" I managed to get out.

"Because I cursed him for turning me in to the army. But Vitya doesn't need an excuse." He gave me a resentful look. "As long as you and your mother live in style, why should you care what your estate manager does? He sends you money. That's all that matters to you." With that he went back into the cottage, slamming the door behind him. The old woman began to moan again.

That night I tried to tell Mama what I had seen. She wouldn't listen. "Oh, Katya. That is servants' gossip. I don't concern myself with such things. All that must be left up to Vitya and Grishka."

When I saw my pleading would do no good, I decided it was time that I take some responsibility for The Oaks. The following morning I went to see Vitya. The estate manager's office was in one wing of the estate. Vitya sat in a large leather swivel chair at a desk overflowing with ruled ledgers. When he saw me, he put on a smile, but his eyes were cold. "Well, Katya, to what do I owe the honor of this visit?"

After a deep breath, I said, "Vitya, does Stepan really have to go into the army? Couldn't they take someone else?" At once I lost heart, for I saw from his expression that he guessed I had served as a messenger between Nina and Stepan.

After a minute Vitya said, "Come, Katya, sit here." He got up from his leather chair and motioned me to take his place.

Frightened, I shook my head.

"Now, come. You have nothing to be afraid of."
He reached out for me and when I resisted, he

clamped his fingers around my arm until it hurt, forcing me into his chair. "There, now, you are the estate manager." He pushed the ruled ledgers at me. "You decide what must be done." When I struggled to get out of the chair, he began to turn it, laughing all the while. Around and around I went until I was dizzy. When I finally escaped, his laughter followed me until it blended with the caws of a flock of crows.

That night Lidya asked me how I got the bruise on my arm. "I fell out of an apple tree," I said.

"Heavens, Katya, you are too old for such unlady-like antics."

The next morning I found my rabbit dead in its cage. Its delicate neck had been rung. I sobbed and sobbed. It was the first deliberate cruelty I had ever known.

I heard Lidya say to Mama, "Who could have done such a heartless thing? Who could possibly have an argument with a small girl?"

Mama told her, "The Baron says the peasants are being incited to acts of violence, but I never thought such a thing would happen here. All the more reason for Vitya to keep the peasants under control."

When Mama questioned me, I only shook my head, afraid she would not believe me and would go to Vitya with my story. He would torment Nina and Stepan and find a more horrible punishment for me.

After that I would not be in the same room with Vitya. The moment I saw him approach, I hurried away. At the end of August, just as we were getting on the train, Vitya handed me a gaily wrapped package. "A belated birthday gift," he said.

With Mama there I had to thank him. Mama urged me to open it. It was a notebook with a pretty rose satin cover and a velvet ribbon to mark my place. But inside it, I saw, the ruled pages were just like those in his ledgers. On the first page Vitya had written: "For the little estate manager."

"Don't look like that, Katya," Mama said. "He is

only teasing you. What a sweet gift. You must begin to keep a diary." As the train pulled out, she said, "I don't know what Baron Nogin has against Vitya. You see what a kind and thoughtful man he is."

CHAPTER FIVE

THE ΛLEXΛNDER PΛLΛCE

Fall–Winter 1913

In September, after many hugs from me, Lidya departed for her sister's home in Moscow, and Mama and I left with Anya, and all our trunks, for the Alexander Palace. It was an hour's train ride to Tsar's Village. The train station there was like a small castle, with chimneys and turrets sticking up from its roof. A carriage sent by the Tsar was waiting to take us to the palace.

The road through the village was lined with the elegant mansions of the Tsar's relatives and ministers of state. At the palace entrance a small army of guards saluted us. Massive wrought-iron gates swung open in welcome. As the gates closed behind us, Misha's words, "You'll be living in a prison," flashed through my mind.

Even with its rows of imposing pillars and its sur-rounding park, the Alexander Palace was not nearly so large and intimidating as the Winter Palace in St. Petersburg.

Mama and I were shown to our rooms, which sur-prised us by being plain and dreary with ugly furniture and faded curtains. Mama loved to have pretty things about her. She always said, "It feeds my soul, Katya." Now, as she looked unhappily around, she whispered to Anya, "I wonder if I dare send for some of our things to freshen up these rooms?"

Though the rooms were plain, there was a fine view from the windows over hundreds of acres of palace gardens, which stretched as far as I could see. An hour later I was exploring the gardens with Stana, who was happy to have me there.

"I have had no one here to run about with," Stana complained. "My sisters, even Marie, say it's not dignified. They only want to sit and gossip and talk about which one of their cousins they will marry one day so they can be empresses like mama and grandmama. Olga had an offer from Prince Carol of Rumania, but she turned him down. I don't want to marry a prince, for they are all vain and used to being pampered. I love horses and want to marry one of those." Stana did not mean a horse but was pointing to the Cossack horsemen patrolling the grounds of the palace. The Cossacks, handsome in scarlet tunics and high fur hats, sat on their fine horses with so much dignity, their mounts might have been thrones. I gave Stana a weak smile, but I knew I would never see a Cossack again without thinking of the men who had raised their whips to the striking women.

Stana led me past rows of marble statues, through miniature Greek temples, and under the thick branches of ancient trees whose foliage had a dusty fall look. Once we stopped to watch the white tail of a shy deer disappear in the distance. Stana paused by a small lake, where a pair of regal swans were gliding. Leaves were floating over the lake's surface. "Soon the lake will freeze," Stana said sadly, "and Alexei will have to wait until next year to sail his boats."

"Why can't he sail them now?" I asked.

"He's too sick," she said. "He bumped his knee, and it's all black and blue and swollen. When I walk by his room, I hear him crying out with the pain. It makes me feel terrible. Mama cries as well, for there is nothing she can do. She has been up night after night with Alexei. Yesterday she called that smelly Grigory Rasputin to come from Moscow. He is here now. His clothes are dirty, and he looks right through you as if your skin were made of glass. But Alexei has been better since Rasputin came, so we have to hold our noses and put up with him. Now, would you like to see the stables?"

"Yes," I said, but I lagged behind her. A carriage had run away with me when I was five, and I was afraid of horses. They were too big, and I didn't like the way they snorted and rolled their eyes and pawed the ground.

There were row after row of stalls, stalls for workhorses, horses to draw carriages, hunters, riding horses, and ponies. "This pony is mine." Stana pointed to a chestnut mare with a white star on her forehead. "I'll tell Papa to give you one, too, so we can ride together."

I took a deep breath and confessed, "I'm afraid of horses."

That did not seem to worry Stana, who only said, "Then you can run alongside me as I ride."

I was glad Misha was not there to hear that. I knew Stana and I were friends, but still she was a grand duchess.

On the way back to the palace we stopped in the orangerie, a glass house filled with flowers and fruit trees. The air was sweet with the fragrance of orange blossoms and gardenias. Tropical birds splashed with bright colors flew about. As if we were in the Garden of Eden, Stana plucked ripe figs and clusters of rosy red grapes for us to nibble on.

I could have stayed there forever, but Stana said, "Come and I'll show you my room. I share it with Marie."

Their room was even plainer than the ones Mama and I had been given. I thought of how Mama had said the Empress did not want to spoil the girls.

"Do you have as nice a room as this in your home in St. Petersburg?" Stana asked.

I did not know how to answer, for my room at the mansion had silk curtains, satin comforters, and on the walls flowered wallpaper, pretty paintings, and a mirror framed in gold. I had shelves of dolls in French gowns made by Madame LaMott and a dollhouse with a little tank so that real water came from the faucets.

Stana's room had folding cots and thin mattresses.

The bed was covered with a simple cotton bed-spread. There were faded cotton curtains at the windows. There was no comfortable chair to curl up in, but only a straight wooden one. I saw a few dolls and, instead of pretty pictures on the walls, only icons with solemn saints staring down at us. Swallowing my pride, I spoke a *vranyo*. "No," I said, telling a little white lie, "my room is also nice, but not so nice as yours."

Stana picked up a book that lay on a bedside table. "I'm glad you'll be doing lessons with me. Our tutor, Pierre Gilliard, is Swiss. He's very distinguished and reads us French poetry. We're all in love with him. My worst subject is mathematics. My sisters are ahead of me, and I'm always last with answers. Promise you won't tell the answers before me."

I promised.

While the bedrooms were plain, the state rooms of the palace were lavish with gilt furniture, silken draperies, and thick carpets. The rooms were warmed with porcelain stoves, set tier upon tier, like frosted wedding cakes. Posted at every door, and at all the stairways, were armed sentries. Their unsmiling faces made me nervous, but Stana ran by them as if they were so many statues.

Unlike the formal state rooms, the rooms where the imperial family lived, except their bedrooms, were cozy with stuffed furniture covered in flowered chintzes and lots of pillows and family photographs and pretty bits and pieces set about.

Olga, Tatiana, and Marie were already at the tea table when we joined them. A moment later Empress Alexandra came into the room, with Mama walking a little behind her. A man followed them into the room. He was tall and heavily muscled, as if he spent his days at farm work. Rasputin, for I was sure that was who this man was, had flowing hair and a long, heavy beard. He was dressed in the tunic, pants, and boots of a peasant. Stana was right. His clothes were rumpled and soiled. I wondered how he dared go before the Empress dressed like that. His eyes were a grayish blue and almost transparent. You looked into them as you would look into clear, deep water. I was so fascinated with him, I nearly forgot my manners. Quickly I sprang out of my chair to curtsy to the Empress.

There were dark circles under her eyes and a heaviness to her walk. She gave me a weary smile. "Ah, Katya. I'm sorry I could not greet you. Stana will have told you that Alexei has not been well, but thanks to our dear friend Father Grigory, he is much better."

The Empress glanced disapprovingly at the tea table, which was set with a simple plate of bread and butter. She summoned one of the footmen. "See that we have some petits fours." She turned back to us. "Father Grigory is very fond of them."

I was delighted, for I was hungry after the long stroll in the garden, and petits fours were my favorite. A silver platter arrived heaped with the little frosted French cakes. The Empress herself took up the platter and put it beside Rasputin's chair. He began to gorge himself on the cakes. One cake after another was crammed into his mouth, and bits of frosting gathered on his beard like flakes of snow on the coat of a furry beast. The girls chatted among themselves, trying not to look at him. Mama and the Empress were talking of some new and outlandish Paris fashion. I could concentrate on nothing but the disappearance of one cake after another into that open mouth. When the whole platter was empty, Rasputin wiped his mouth with the sleeve of his tunic.

"*Khorosho*," he said in approval. He looked in the direction of the footman, but the Empress did not order another platter. Instead she said to Rasputin, "How can I thank you enough, dear friend, for what you have done for Alexei?"

As Rasputin calmly picked crumbs from his beard, I saw him looking at my mother in a very unpleasant way, as if she were delicious enough to devour like one of the petits fours. After a moment he turned to the Empress. "Mama, these are troubling times. You must tell Papa that he should be watchful of Germany."

He had called the Tsar "Papa," and the Empress "Mama"!

It did not seem to bother the Empress, for she merely nodded her approval. "Yes, that is excellent advice, my friend. I promise I'll speak to the Tsar this evening."

Rasputin got up, sending a little shower of crumbs from his lap onto the carpet. He gave Mama another hungry look. "Irina Petrovna," he said to her in honeyed tones, "you must come and visit me one day."

Mama gave him a weak smile.

Unlike everyone else, Rasputin did not back out of the room but turned his back on the Empress and strode away. The Empress appeared undisturbed by this, and the girls were still busy chatting.

Later that evening, when we were alone, I asked Mama, "You won't go and visit Rasputin?"

"Good heavens, no. It is worth a woman's reputation to be seen in that man's apartment."

Startled, I asked, "What do you mean?"

"Never mind, Katya. I shouldn't have spoken."

"He is so rude, and he tries to tell the Tsar what to do, and he turns his back on the Empress."

"Yes, all those things are true, but I believe the Empress would deal with the devil himself if it could spare Alexei pain." After a moment Mama sighed and added, "Perhaps she does."

That night I slept for the first time in my unfamiliar and not too comfortable bed. With no satin comforter, and only a very small porcelain stove to warm the room, I lay awake wishing I were back in St. Petersburg.

In the morning a footman delivered a note addressed to me. "COME AND HAVE LESSONS WITH US AT NINE O'CLOCK. OTMA."

Puzzled, I asked Mama, "Who is Otma?"

"That is how the girls sign, with the first letters of their names: Olga, Tatiana, Marie, and Anastasia."

The schoolroom was furnished with desks, a blackboard, and many maps. Alexei and the girls were studying French with their tutor. Such lessons were very necessary, for among families like ours, French was spoken as often as Russian.

Pierre Gilliard had fine brown hair that curled over his coat collar, a mustache, and hooded brown eyes that looked shyly out at you. His manners were perfect. When we were introduced, I hoped he would kiss my hand, but he didn't. Alexei and the girls hung on his words. As he recited a French poem, the words coming from his lips were like syrup, spooned rather than spoken. Later, when Stana and I did our arithmetic, even the tutor's adding and subtracting of numbers seemed romantic.

I knew the answers to the problems before Stana and longed to show the tutor how well I could do, but I remembered my promise and waited for Stana to answer first. She was far ahead of me in English, though, for she heard it every day. The Tsar spoke Russian to the girls but English to the Empress, who, though she was German, had been brought up in England.

• • •

As the fall passed, I fell into the life of the palace. There was schoolwork during the day, and there were cozy evenings with the imperial family, who enjoyed one another's company. Before I knew it, winter was upon us. One morning Stana pounded at my door. "The pond is frozen! Bring your skates!"

Olga, Tatiana, Marie, Stana, and I, warmly clothed in coats and woolen tams and mittens, glided over the ice and frolicked in the snow. Alexei watched us wistfully, for he was not allowed to risk an injury. He had to be content with our pulling him about on a sleigh or allowing him to pelt us with snowballs. The snow made the older girls forget their dignity. They chased Stana and me, their hair tumbling over their shoulders. Suddenly, as he often did, the Tsar appeared with his camera to take our pictures. I knew that later he would carefully paste the photographs into an album filled with hundreds of photographs of the Duchesses and Alexei.

That evening I went along to a performance of the ballet, which we often attended at the theater in Tsar's Village. I sat in the imperial box, and when the audience and even the performers bowed to our box, I could almost hear Misha saying, "So, Katya, now you allow people to bow down to you."

I soon forgot about Misha and lost myself in my favorite ballet, *Lebedinoye Ozero, Swan Lake*. When the swan died, we all cried, except for Stana, who giggled because the feathers kept falling off the swan's costume. "It's molting," she said, giggling.

When we returned to the palace, I sat up with Stana and her sisters talking about the dancers. We kicked off our shoes and danced about on our tiptoes, humming the music. We all longed to be ballerinas, but Tatiana was the only one among us with the needed slim, graceful figure. No matter how the rest of us held in our stomachs, or arched our necks, or wound our hair into prim chignons, we knew we would never have danced well enough to join the corps de ballet.

The ballerinas were the most famous women in Russia. Everything they did was talked of. I would overhear Anya and Mama gossiping about the dancers, and I would pass the gossip on to Stana. We knew with whom the ballerinas were in love and who was in love with them. When a great bouquet of roses was thrown upon the stage, we would whisper, "That is from Grand Duke Mikhail," or whoever was the current lover of the ballerina.

Though Stana had become like a sister to me, I grew close to the other Grand Duchesses as well. Olga had her own ideas about things and often went off by herself. If the Empress corrected her, even over a small thing, she would sulk. Tatiana had an even disposition and was always the first to make peace among us. Marie was almost too good to be true. She was warm-hearted and eager to give a compliment on a new dress. She openhandedly shared everything that belonged to her. Stana was more fun-loving and more high-spirited, but her practical jokes were sometimes cruel, and I winced when she played them on the servants, who could not complain.

If Stana had been one of my old friends, I would have scolded her for such behavior, but one did not scold a duchess. I knew that, in spite of the girls' friendship, and all their kindnesses toward me, we would never be equals.

We seldom had conversations about what was going on in the country. I had not forgotten the children who were working in the government paper factory. I had not given up my idea of finding a way to let the Tsar know about the factory. One afternoon I tried to tell Stana about the children and about the strikes, but she wouldn't listen.

"That is just propaganda," she said. "It's all lies told by the revolutionaries."

"No, Stana," I said, "I saw it with my own eyes."

Stana grew angry. "You are our guest here, Katya. You have no right to say things against my papa."

With that she strode away. The rest of the day she ignored me. After that I knew I must keep my thoughts about such things to myself.

By breakfast the next day Stana was as friendly as ever. It was a mild December day, and the Tsar had ridden off in the early-morning darkness to go hunting. When he returned in the afternoon, he was hungry and refreshed, his face rosy and his eyes bright. Stana and I were allowed to go to the scullery, where heaps of grouse and rabbits were being prepared. We begged for some of the pretty feathers. One of the huntsmen offered us the bloody stump of a rabbit tail. All I could think of was my Angora rabbit, strangled by Vitya. I ran horrified from the scullery. When Stana asked what was wrong, I only shook my head. I belonged to the Duchesses—but not all of me.

We began to prepare for Christmas by attending church every day, for the Empress Alexandra was very devout. I knew she prayed fervently to God and to the saints painted on her icons to make Alexei better.

On Christmas Eve a huge tree went up in the palace hall. Scrambling up and down ladders, the girls and I decorated the tree with fruits and candies, gilded nuts, and small presents. On each tree branch we put a tiny wax taper in a silver holder. When at last the tree was decorated, we were sent away while two footmen lit the candles. The electric lights in the hall were turned off, and we returned to be dazzled by the shining tree, its hundreds of small flames alive in the darkness.

As midnight approached, we were carried in sleighs through the snow to church. After the service we exchanged Christmas greetings: "*S rozhdestvom Khristovom*," we called to one another. The Tsar and the Empress stood in the church entrance while everyone else came up to bow to the Tsar and kiss the Empress's hand. Finally we returned to the palace for a huge feast. There were twelve dishes to remind us of the twelve apostles. The feast ended with honey cake and a crystal bowl of dried fruit stewed in wine and liquor. Stana and I disgraced ourselves by taking second helpings and then pretending we were drunk.

On Christmas morning we all exchanged gifts. The girls had only a small allowance. Their presents were gifts they made themselves. My allowance was more generous, but Mama said I must do as the girls did. For Olga, who loved poetry, I copied out five poems by a French poet she admired. For Tatiana, who took pride in her embroidery, I sewed a needle case. For Marie, who liked to paint pretty pictures, I made a scrapbook of flowers cut from Mama's magazines for her to copy. Stana was always losing her mittens. I knitted her a pair and put strings on them to go through her coat sleeves.

Mama and I were remembered by everyone. The girls made presents for me. The Tsar and Empress gave me a gold locket in the shape of a four-leaf clover. It was made by the famous court jeweler Fabergé, and each loop of the clover held a picture of one of the girls.

Alexei was showered with gifts. He received books and puzzles and intricately carved wooden villages with trains to run through them. His favorite present was a board game called War in Europe. It had clever cardboard cutouts of soldiers, cannons, houses on fire, mounted cavalry officers, and hospital wagons. Alexei loved everything about soldiers. When he received a Cossack's uniform made in his size, he put it on and would not take it off. "You'll see," he announced, "someday when I am better, I will lead a regiment as Papa did."

I saw the Empress turn away so that Alexei should not see the tears in her eyes.

In the evening we went for a troika ride into the countryside. The carriages, each driven by three horses abreast, glided over the snow. The bells on their harnesses jangled. Netting stretched across the front of the carriage protected us from lumps of hard snow kicked up by the horses. The steam from the horses' nostrils made little white clouds in the night air. Overhead the stars sparkled like chips of ice, but we were warm and snug, wrapped in bearskin robes, our feet resting on little stoves that held heated coals.

Mama and the Empress remained at home, but the Tsar accompanied us, bringing with him a brace of Cossacks to ride alongside his troika. There was no formality. The girls and Alexei called out to the Tsar as if he were just an ordinary papa.

"See the moon shadows on the snow, Papa," Marie called.

"Yes, yes, my dear, like stripes on the zebra we saw in the zoo."

At such a moment as that, or later that evening when the Tsar sat and read to us in his pleasant, soft voice, or when he played a game of dominoes with Alexei, careful to let Alexei win, I felt if I told him about the boys and girls who picked rags, he would find a way to help them. Then I remembered how angry Stana had been with me when I had tried to tell her. I could not help recalling Misha's words: "The Tsar prefers to close his eyes to such matters."

CHAPTER SIX

A VOYAGE ON THE STANDART

Spring–Summer 1914

In May the Tsar and his family made their usual trip south to their palace in the Crimea. There, on the Black Sea, it would already be summer. "Everything will be in bloom," Stana said.

I believed her, for already armfuls of lilacs and roses, sent north by railway from the Crimea, filled the palace. Mama and I would not go along, but soon after the imperial family returned, we would accompany them on their private yacht for a cruise. I kissed all the girls good-bye, giving two kisses to Stana, who promised to let me read all about the trip in the diary she kept.

Mama and I returned to the Zhukovsky mansion. Although things were more comfortable, and the teas included cakes and sweets, I missed my new family. When I heard the scripture read at St. Isaac's, I blinked away tears of loneliness at the prophet Isaiah's words: "Kings shall be thy nursing fathers." I had begun to think of the Tsar as a father.

It was only when Misha, on a week's vacation from the military academy, joined us that I cheered up. I hardly recognized him. His blond curls had been clipped. His cadet's uniform made him look older and gave him a soldierly bearing. Mama was delighted and kissed him warmly on both cheeks.

I was a little intimidated and hung back until he grinned and said, "Well, Katya, have you been so surrounded by handsome palace guards that you have no kiss to spare for me?"

At that I knew I had my old Misha back. I threw

my arms about him and tried to crowd into an hour the telling of all the things that had happened to me since I had last seen him. It was only when we were alone after dinner that I gave him a chance to talk about himself. "Tell me what the academy is like," I begged.

"Up at five in the morning, cold baths, cold porridge, cold tea. We sit in a classroom, and besides mathematics, languages, and military law, we learn how to move great armies about as if they were chessmen. In the afternoon we make our horses jump over fences, and then we run at one another with bayonets."

"It sounds horrible."

"Actually it was not so bad until recently, when our instructors began to take it all a little too seriously. They want us to be prepared. There is a rumor that our class will be graduated a year early."

"What do you mean prepared? Why should you be graduated early?" I asked.

He gave me a condescending look. "Have you

learned where Serbia is in your geography lessons?"

"Don't patronize me, Misha. Of course I know where it is. It's all the way at the bottom of Europe, where Greece and Italy are, near the Adriatic Sea. It's next to the Austro-Hungarian Empire."

"Good enough. I can tell you your beloved Tsar knows where it is. The Tsar has been making mischief down there, encouraging the Serbs to cause trouble for Austria. There is talk that the Tsar is giving money to support the Serbian terrorists."

At once I was on the defensive. "Impossible. I don't believe you. Why ever would he want to do that?" I asked. I dreaded having to hear Misha start in on his criticism of the Tsar.

"It keeps Austria busy and weakens her," Misha said. "The Tsar doesn't want the armies of Germany and Austria nipping at his heels. He wants them facing south toward Serbia and not north toward Russia. The Tsar knows Russia is not prepared for another war."

"Misha," I scolded, "you have only just come home and already you are saying nasty things about the Tsar. You are ruining our reunion, and you will get into trouble for saying such things." I wanted to be loyal to the Tsar, yet it was hard to make myself believe that Misha would invent such things.

Misha's voice had been light and teasing. Suddenly he became solemn. "You are right when you say it is dangerous to say such things. The Tsar is cracking down on anyone who opposes him. It was one thing when he exiled hotheads like Lenin and Stalin. They only want to stir up trouble. Lenin would love to see a war between Russia and Austria. But now one of my close friends from the university has been sent off to Siberia. If there is a war, the Tsar will declare anyone who opposes him a traitor to Russia and have him shot."

I was close to tears. "How can you say such things, Misha? I see you for the first time in months, and you spoil everything with your gloomy imaginings. I didn't hear a word about war at the Alexander Palace, and I saw the Tsar nearly every day."

"Be sensible, Katya. Do you imagine the Tsar sits at the tea table and asks his daughters and their friend if he should sign a treaty with France or England? Or if he should deploy a division of his army here or there?"

When he saw the crushed look on my face, Misha relented. "Forgive me, Katya. You are right. I should not be talking about such things. It is only that I can't discuss them at the military academy, or they would throw me out." Suddenly he grinned. "That would not be so bad. The only thing that keeps me from it is that the Grand Duke Nikolai would have me shot, which would make your mama cry. You, no doubt, would rejoice."

After that, Misha was in a good humor, and the week of his vacation became very pleasant. He took me to see a play by the great writer Chekhov, and he bought me a box of chocolates to keep me awake, for on the stage nothing much went on except talk. Much better, we went to the ballet to see *The Nutcracker*. I had played some of the music on the piano. Afterward he took me to a fashionable café on the Nevsky and bought me as much cake as I could eat.

It was only because I had the reunion with the imperial family and the voyage on their yacht to look forward to that I could bear to part with Misha. As we said good-bye, I begged him, "Promise to let your hair grow again."

"Yes, yes, I will tell my commanding officer that my cousin respectfully requests a return of my charming curls, and he will certainly make an exception for me." And so, laughing, we parted.

In July Mama and I readied ourselves to join the Tsar and his family aboard the imperial yacht. The yacht, one of many the Tsar owned, was the size of a small village and so large I did not see how it could float. It was festooned with scores of bright flags and pennants. Alexei could explain the meaning of nearly every one.

Our staterooms were more comfortable than our bedrooms in the palace, and each one had a round porthole so that the Baltic Sea looked in at us like a great watery eye. The decks were as wide as streets. Lounge chairs with crisp white linen covers were set out on the decks. There was even a billiard room. In the dining room sailors took over the duties of footmen. Because of their military discipline they were more skillful and deft than footmen, especially when the yacht rolled and they had to catch sliding dishes.

A navy band played music in the evenings, and at teatime a group of old men played balalaikas. The balalaika is an instrument that always makes me sad. Sadder even than their music was Empress Alexandra's piano playing in the lounge. As we girls raced up and down the decks, or sat in the lounge chairs reading, we could hear her at the keyboard, playing Chopin. She played beautifully, but all her unhappiness over Alexei, who was once again ill with an injury to his knee, went into the music. Though I never saw her cry, it sounded as though the keys of the piano were drenched with tears. She could not call upon Rasputin. Stana had whispered to me that Rasputin had been stabbed by a jealous woman and had nearly died. "Women won't leave Rasputin alone. He has sweethearts all over Russia," Stana said. "Only we can't say that in front of Mama, who will not listen to anything against him."

Rasputin sent a reply to the Empress's plea to help Alexei. He wrote he was still recovering from "a mad-woman's attack," but the Empress was not to worry. He was sure Alexei would be fine.

Rasputin proved right. A few days after he sent his message, Alexei began to recover. The Empress told the Tsar, "Father Grigory has such wisdom. If only you would listen to his advice on affairs of state." At this the girls rolled their eyes. A thin smile appeared on the Tsar's face, and he hastily changed the subject.

While he could be strict and even hard with those who worked on the boat, he never raised his voice to the Empress.

The yacht sailed along the coast of Finland, which belonged to Russia. Much of the coast was rocky, wild, and dense with birch and pine forests. If the day was pleasant, the Tsar would order a tender to take us ashore. Accompanying us were sailors lugging huge picnic baskets. While the Empress and Mama stayed aboard the yacht with Alexei, the Tsar took the girls and me for rambles through kilometers of deep woods.

Though I was pleased to be on solid ground again, I was a little afraid of so much uninhabited woodland. I worried that behind each tree lurked a bear or a wolf. When nothing ate me, I gained courage, and soon I was running freely about the woods with Stana. The Tsar took great pleasure in instructing us.

"No! Don't pick the orange-and-yellow mushrooms," he warned us. "They are poisonous." He showed us shaggy mushrooms and fat white ones.

"These can be safely gathered." He even let us take them back to the yacht to be cooked in butter and served on toast with sour cream, and no one died.

Marie carried her watercolors with her. She painted the white birches against the dark-green pines. Olga sat happily on a moss-covered log, staring out at the sea and writing poems in her diary. Tatiana loved to observe the birds. The Tsar encouraged her to keep a list and a description of every bird she saw. Later, when we returned to the yacht, the Tsar would take out a large book, and together they would search out the birds' names.

Stana and I set ourselves no artistic or scientific tasks. We hid among the birches and ran along the shore, finding pretty stones and picking wildflowers to take back to cheer the Empress. Still, the Tsar made little lessons in geology and botany from our foraging, so that in no time we learned the proper names for our stones and flowers. Though we did not dare say so to the Tsar, Stana and I thought many of the Latin names ugly and gave the flowers secret names like String of Pearls and Old Lace.

Alexei, who was still recovering, was left behind on these excursions. The sailors, feeling sorry for him, dressed him up in a sailor's uniform and gave him a dark-blue sailor's cap with the name of the yacht, *Standart*, in gold letters. When he was well enough, they carried him all over the yacht. "The captain let me steer," he boasted, "and the navigator let me plot our course."

At the end of each day the sailors would lower the ship's flag. The sun's golden circle would disappear into the water, and we would all fall silent while the voices of the sailors singing the Lord's Prayer were carried out over the sea.

Four days passed pleasantly. When we weren't ashore, we found things to do on the yacht. We had even brought our roller skates along, and the five of us skated around and around the decks, shined to a smoothness each morning by the sailors.

One afternoon we girls begged the band to play dance music for us. We put on our best summer dresses and coaxed the officers to wear their dress uniforms. With the Tsar and the Empress and Mama looking on, tolerant smiles on their faces, the officers whirled us around the deck while the band played Strauss waltzes. Olga and Tatiana flirted with the young officers. Marie and Stana and I were stuck with the older officers. Mine had a mustache like a walrus and smelled of cigars.

The band was so loud and lively, we didn't hear the official-looking motor launch until it was nearly alongside the yacht. A man stood in the bow of the launch looking so impatient that I was afraid at any moment he might jump overboard and swim the last few yards. The man, who was dressed formally in a black suit, regarded the ladder that had been lowered for him with dismay.

"Ivan Ivanovich," the Tsar called out. "Don't be a coward. Just scramble up."

"It's Papa's private secretary," Stana told me. "It must be something important." The Tsar did not like to be interrupted with state business when he was vacationing on his yacht.

The two men disappeared into the Tsar's office. A half hour later the Tsar joined us. He was pale. He sank down onto one of the lounge chairs and looked about him as if he did not know where he was. At last he said, "You may as well all know. There has been a terrible tragedy in Serbia."

The Empress leaned forward. "What is it?"

"The nephew and heir of Emperor Franz Joseph of Austria has been murdered by Serbian terrorists in Sarajevo. His wife is dead as well."

The Empress put her hands to her chest as if she were keeping her heart from leaping out.

"How horrible," Mama said.

"Why ever would they do such a thing, Papa?" Olga asked. There were tears in her eyes.

"The Serbian terrorists want to force Austria to give up some of her Slavic countries," the Tsar replied.

All I could think of were Misha's words, "The Tsar has been making mischief down there, giving the Serbian terrorists money and encouraging them to wander about causing trouble for Austria." If that were true, had the Tsar ever thought his money would pay for a horror like this?

"Should we end our cruise, my dear?" the Empress asked. She must not have been thinking of our presence, for never before had I heard her address the Tsar so informally.

The Tsar looked about him as if the answer might have been misplaced on a chair or table. After a moment he said, "No. There is no need for that. It is terrible for Franz Joseph to lose the heir to his throne, but Austria will not make war over it."

The cruise continued, but there were no more rambles with the Tsar. Several times a day motorboats sped up to our yacht with the latest news dispatches. The Tsar said, "Austria holds Serbia responsible for the assassination. We can only pray Austria is not so foolish as to go to war with Serbia, for she'll take Germany with her."

A cloud hung over the rest of the voyage. The Empress spent most of her time with Alexei, who had still not completely recovered from his knee injury. The Tsar strode about the deck with a preoccupied look. The old men played sadder and sadder songs on their balalaikas. Even Stana's high spirits were quashed. In spite of the Tsar's reassurances, it felt as if a dangerous beast, a hungry lion or tiger, were loose on the boat and might at any moment leap out at us.

At the end of our voyage we did not return at once to Tsar's Village but remained in St. Petersburg, for the President of France was making a state visit and must be entertained. Still the beast continued to creep about. Austria, furious over the assassination of its crown prince, made impossible demands of Serbia, hoping to provoke it into war. At first Serbia refused the demands, but Serbia could see that Austria wanted to invade their country. So they accepted the demands, hoping to keep Austria out. Still Austria was not satisfied. Austria began shooting at Serbia.

As far as I could see, all of Europe was like a children's playground, with everyone choosing sides. Austria and Germany were best friends. France, England, Russia, and Serbia were the other team. If Serbia were attacked, Russia had promised, we would come to Serbia's aid. All at once everyone hated everyone else. In St. Petersburg, right across from St. Isaac's Cathedral, a mob attacked the German embassy.

Signs posted along the Nevsky read: *His Majesty the Emperor has been graciously pleased to order the army and the fleet to be placed on a war footing.*

The word "*voina*," war, frightened me. When we were alone in our rooms in the Winter Palace, I asked Mama, "What do all these preparations mean?"

Mama sighed. "I'm afraid, my darling, that they mean war."

I could not help remembering that Papa had been killed in Russia's last war. I thought of Misha in the army and prayed that war would not come.

It did come. One of the Tsar's cousins, Kaiser Wilhelm, the Emperor of Germany, demanded that the Tsar stop preparing for war. Though the Tsar cut back, some preparations continued. The Tsar said Russia must be prepared. When he saw the preparations continuing, the German Kaiser declared war on Russia.

We were all at dinner waiting for the Tsar to join us. It was August first, my fourteenth birthday, and a dinner was planned with my favorite dessert, blackberry ice cream specially made by Toma from fragrant wild blackberries.

It was unusual for the Tsar to come late to a meal. They say punctuality is the virtue of kings, and so it was with the Tsar. If someone was a moment or two late, he pulled out his heavy gold pocket watch and looked at it, even shaking it, as if it must be the watch and could not possibly be someone's carelessness. His lateness at the dinner table worried the Empress. When at last he walked into the dining room, it was with a heavy step. His voice was hoarse, as if the words scorched his throat. "Germany and Austria have declared war on Russia."

The Empress and the girls all burst into tears. "This is the end of everything," the Empress moaned.

I cried with the others, but I must confess part of the sadness was because in all the excitement my birthday had been forgotten. It was not until Misha's letter came that I began to understand what war meant.

• • •

Moscow
August 10, 1914

Dear Katya,

They have pushed up our graduation so
that I am now a full-fledged officer in the
Tsar's army. Today I have received my orders.
I will soon be posted to the Second Army
Corps. I sometimes wonder why I am
fighting in this army. I don't see why we are
at war. This is an old men's quarrel brought
about by emperors and not the people. The
hothead Lenin is as anxious for the war as
the Tsar. Between the two of them they will
kill Russia.

Yet I will fight. I suppose it is because I
love Russia. Still, I will not give up my
dreams to free our country one day. Kerensky,
the revolutionary I admire above all others,
said, "We will defend our country and then

*we will liberate it." Those are my thoughts
exactly.*

> *You are not to worry about me, Katya.
> And don't write any more letters to the Tsar.
> He's getting all the bad advice he needs.*

*Affectionately,
Misha*

Now at last I understood what war meant. It
meant I might never see Misha again.

CHAPTER SEVEN

WAR COMES TO THE PALACE

Summer 1914–Fall 1915

In St. Petersburg a hundred thousand people gathered around the column with the angel in Palace Square. They were there to show their support for the war. Alexei, too ill to join the family, was left behind. To amuse him I found bits of yellow cloth, and together we fashioned a flag and on it, using black ink, we drew the imperial double-headed eagle. After proudly pinning it up in his room, Alexei brought out his war game. Though I had little heart for it, I agreed to play. Polite as always, Alexei said, "First I'll take Russia's part. Then we'll change off, for each of us must have a chance to beat the Germans."

When the family returned from the square, Stana was flushed with excitement. "Katya, there were so many people! They shouted out their love for Papa and fell to their knees to show their devotion to him. Papa looked splendid in his uniform. He took an oath before the miraculous icon that saved Russia from Napoleon. Raising his right hand, he pledged: 'I will not make peace as long as a single enemy remains on Russian soil.' Oh, Katya, you never heard such cheering or saw so many tears. We wept too, even Papa and Mama."

Russian soldiers marched into Germany. In St. Petersburg thousands of volunteer soldiers paraded with their regiments. The prospekt was lined with cheering crowds throwing flowers at the soldiers. Only when I looked closely did I see the weeping wives and mothers of the departing men. After that I could not cheer.

Though the Empress had been born in Germany, I saw that her whole heart now belonged to Russia. She wanted nothing more than a victory for Russia. At the palace she put us to work knitting wool socks for the soldiers. "But Mama," Stana said, "it's so hot out. Why must we make socks of wool? Surely the war will be over by the winter."

Alexei said, "No, no. The war must go on until I can join the army."

"You are both mistaken, my dears," the Empress said. "Stana, I fear the soldiers will still be fighting in cold weather. Germany is a large country, and there is Austria besides. But Alexei, sweetheart, much as you may want to be a soldier, do not wish for a long war. We must pray the war will be over as soon as possible. There is cheering now, and there will be many brave deeds, but there is also pain and suffering. We must be prepared for that."

We did prepare. The linen sheets with their imperial crest, still smelling of lavender, were taken down from the closet shelves of the palace. The Empress took a deep breath and began to rip the sheets into strips. There was something terrible about the sound of the linen ripping, as if more than the imperial sheets were being torn apart. From the strips the girls and I made bandages, hundreds of them.

Tatiana, who had a soft heart and would weep over a wounded bird, asked, "Mama, why so many bandages? Will they all be needed?"

In a gentle voice the Empress said, "We pray that they will not, Tatiana, but it is better to be prepared."

All the time I made the bandages, I thought of the weeping wives and mothers. Always I thought of Misha. I did indeed pray that the bandages would never be needed and wondered why there had to be wars. Why couldn't countries settle their quarrels as simply as Stana and I settled who would get the larger piece of cake—one person cut the cake, the other person got first choice. If the Tsar was so powerful, why could he not have stopped the fighting? I did not see how he could sleep at night for thinking of all the soldiers on the battlefields.

In spite of the war our life went on as usual. It was important that the imperial family show itself going about its duties, so that the Russian people would feel confident. We attended theater and ballet performances. Stana and her sisters and I gathered in one another's rooms to try on our newest dresses and hats. I had grown-up hats now instead of straw sailors. The hats, with their wide brims wrapped with yards and yards of veiling and decorated with silk flowers, looked as if they had come from a confectionery shop. Yet even as I put on my new elegant dresses and hats, a small voice inside me asked how I could rejoice in my clothes when soldiers were marching off to war.

Not all the clothes were frivolous. Both Olga and Tatiana were made honorary members of regiments and given uniforms to wear on special occasions. Olga was the honorary commander-in-chief of the Third Hussars Regiment. Tatiana was honorary commander-in-chief of the Eighth Lancers Regiment. Olga's skirt was bright red, and her jacket was blue with golden fastenings and large pearls for buttons. There was a high military collar and a smart cap with a black patent-leather visor. Tatiana's regimentals were navy blue with gold trimmings, brass buttons, and shoulder tabs.

"Mama," Marie and Stana begged, "why can't we have uniforms?"

Alexei was angry as well, for now he was not the only one with a uniform. "They are girls," he complained. "Why should they look like soldiers?"

The Empress tried to soothe him. "Now, sweetheart, don't take on so. You will only make yourself sick. Someday you will be in the real army like your papa, but your mama and your sisters will not."

I did not know about Olga and Tatiana, but from what I had seen of the Empress, I thought she would make a very good soldier, even a general.

By the middle of August we were back at the

Alexander Palace. On August fifteenth, the Feast of the Assumption, when the ascension of the Virgin Mary into heaven was celebrated, we heard the first bad news of the war. Because it was a fast day, we did without milk or cream at breakfast. When the Tsar looked about for the cream, Alexei was quick to say, "*Nyet*, Papa, you have forgotten what day this is."

The Tsar smiled at Alexei. "So I have, Son. I'm afraid my mind is on other things." He began to sort through a stack of papers. As he turned them over, his face became more and more grave. Though we tried not to show it, we were all watching him. At last he stood up to leave.

Almost as an afterthought he turned to us. "There is worrying news from the front. We must not forget our brave soldiers in our prayers." With that he left us.

Indeed, the newspapers, which had been so encouraging, were now gloomy. The Russian army had marched into German territory. German soldiers had fled. But once the Russian army was well into enemy territory and far from the supplies it needed, the German army had turned and attacked. My heart sank, for I had not prepared myself for bad news. I learned the sad story a few weeks later in a letter from Misha. The letter did not come through the mail but was delivered by a soldier from Misha's regiment. As I read the letter I understood why. Even I knew that an army censor would never have allowed such a letter to be sent.

· *September 3, 1914*

My Dear Katya,

I cannot tell you where I am, but I am alive and thankful for it. I have a small wound of no importance that is keeping me in the hospital, but I hope to be back in the fighting soon. The war is a disaster. General Samsonov has shot himself to death in despair over our defeat.

*Recruits are sent to the front lines
with no training. We have run out of
ammunition. Soldiers have to wait unarmed
until they can pick up the rifles of their fallen
comrades. The German cannons cover
thirteen kilometers, but ours cover only six.
We go days without food. The generals have
no idea what they are doing. I have it from a
good source that we even send secret
communications over the telegraph without
using a code! The Germans pick up our
signals and know our next move as quickly
as we do!*

*Still, fool that I am, I will go back. Killing
a Russian soldier isn't enough; you have to
knock him down as well!*

Affectionately,
Misha

Misha wounded! I read and reread his letter. How

could the Tsar let his soldiers go without food and rifles? What had the Tsar thought when he heard his own general had killed himself? What if he didn't know? What if it was like the child ragpickers all over again? I remembered how Misha had said the Tsar preferred to close his eyes to unpleasant truths.

I was afraid to repeat Misha's words, but when we were alone, I asked Stana, "Why should so many men be injured and killed?"

"It's very sad," she answered. "Still, Russians should be proud to die for their country."

I told myself Stana could say that because no one she knew had been hurt.

That soon changed. The imperial family itself began to suffer losses. Friends and relatives of the Tsar and Empress were wounded or missing. Before, as we knitted or rolled our bandages, we had chatted and gossiped. Now we were so silent at our work that the Empress asked the girls to take turns reading aloud from foreign novels.

"It will pass the time," the Empress said, "and improve your French and English." So we rolled our bandages while listening to *David Copperfield* and *Les Misérables*. We held our breath as Jean Valjean hid from his stalker in the Paris sewers. We cried as Dora died in the arms of David Copperfield. While there was tragedy all around us, we escaped to the tragedies in books, which went away when the books were closed.

Stana refused to read any bad news about the war, but each day I made myself read the newspapers, where horrors of the war were revealed. Twenty thousand Russian soldiers had been killed. Seventy thousand had been taken prisoner by the Germans. In the newspapers they were only numbers, but I thought again of the tears of the mothers and wives. This was all happening because one country wanted a piece of another country. I thought that if I were the Tsar, I would call all my soldiers home.

To take care of the wounded soldiers, the Empress

and the Tsar turned the Catherine Palace into a hospital. The Catherine Palace, only a short distance from the Alexander Palace, was a strange place for a hospital. There were marble floors, decorated ceilings, priceless paintings, rooms covered with exotic Chinese wallpapers, and a great ballroom walled in mirrors. The hundreds of little gilded chairs in the ballroom were pushed aside, the mirrors covered, and row after row of iron cots moved in. The palace looked like a woman wearing an elegant hat with a dress of coarse homespun.

The Empress and all the ladies-in-waiting, along with Olga and Tatiana, took a course in nursing. When the course was completed, they were fitted with nurses' uniforms: long gray gowns with headdresses that covered their hair and a part of their forehead. They looked like nuns. They were soon working in the wards, where Olga and Tatiana washed and bandaged the soldiers who were brought in, bloody, filthy, and infested with lice. The sisters never complained, and they even fell a little in love with the young wounded officers under their care.

The Empress and Mama helped in the operating rooms where amputations were carried on. Olga whispered to Stana and me, "Mama took an arm from the surgeon after an amputation." The Empress brought flowers for the wounded soldiers and sat by their bedsides for hours at a time, reading to them. Each evening when the Empress and Mama returned from the hospital, their uniforms were soiled with dirt and blood.

I saw a change in Mama. She no longer let Anya fuss with her hair. She gave no thought to her clothes. Her work at the hospital was her whole life. In the past she had curled up next to me before I fell asleep, curious about my day and whispering bits of palace gossip. Now, at the end of a day in the hospital, she was too tired to do more than pick at dinner and fall into bed.

I begged Mama to let Stana and me help at the hospital. Mama said we were too young. I did not think that I could spend my days idly while soldiers were dying. More and more I was coming to hate the war. I begged Stana to ask her mother's permission for us to go to the hospital, but Stana only shook her head. "Mama will only say '*nyet*.'"

Without a word to Mama, who would surely have forbidden it, I went myself to the Empress. "Madame," I begged, "it is so hard doing nothing. Surely there is some small way Stana and I can help at the hospital?"

There were tears in the Empress's eyes, "Oh, Katya, it is very sad there, and you and Stana are so young."

"There are soldiers dying who are not much older than Stana and I are." At once I regretted my words. Surely she would think I was impudent. She might even think I was criticizing the Tsar.

Instead she put her hand on mine, so gently I hardly felt it. "I'll have a word with the head nurse, Katya, and we will see."

A word from the Empress was law. We were allowed to go to the Catherine Palace. Though we had no uniforms, Stana and I visited the wards of the recovering soldiers. We wrote letters for them and gave them drinks of water. We played cards and chess with them and laughed when they teased us, calling us mischievous angels. Though I tried my best to be cheerful in the wards, I began to have nightmares, which I kept from Mama, for I knew if I told her, she would not let me return to the wards.

While I was with the soldiers, I tried not to notice their missing limbs. One young sergeant had lost his right arm. He was Misha's age, with Misha's yellow curls. I was drawn to him and often wheeled him about the palace gardens. His name was Yuri, and he came from a small village near Rostov, sixteen hundred kilometers south of St. Petersburg.

When I asked him about his village, he said, "As a boy I was lucky. When I was ten years old, the aristocrat who owned the estate on which my father worked apprenticed me to the blacksmith. I would have been set for life, but when the war came, our master said we must do the patriotic thing and enlist in the army. I was proud to do it." He looked down at his empty coat sleeve. "God willing, my master will find some other work for me."

"Perhaps you could get work here," I suggested, thinking I might speak to the Empress, for several of the palace servants had gone to war, and replacements might be needed.

"This place? Never. Never to hear the dove in the morning and the whippoorwill in the evening? Never see the wheat turn golden and the buckwheat flower? I can live without my arm, but I cannot live without the land." After a moment he asked curiously, "Tell me, I have seen you writing letters for the soldiers and reading books to them, so even though you are a girl, you must be educated. Can you explain to me why we are fighting this war?"

I was asking the same question of myself. As each

day another bed was filled, as the newspapers told of one defeat after another, as the Tsar looked gloomier and gloomier, I wanted to ask the Tsar why he didn't end the war. I knew I daren't say that to Yuri. I only shook my head.

Yuri nodded, as if there were some questions that no one could answer.

We knew the soldiers wished to spare us and were careful not to tell us stories that would disturb us, but as the weeks and months of the war wore on, we could not escape the troubling news.

In the classroom Pierre showed us how all the rest of Europe, and America and China as well, could be tucked inside Russia's boundaries. "Russia's great size is a problem," he explained. "Russian trains with military supplies have to stretch long distances, while the German trains have only short distances to travel to reach their soldiers."

I saw how critical the newspapers were of the Tsar. There were reports that factories were not turning out enough ammunition, and just as Misha had written, soldiers were having to fight with the guns of their fallen comrades. England and France, who had joined us in the war, could not help us, for they were fighting for their lives. It was rumored that the German army was at the gates of Paris.

The newspapers began to warn of food shortages, for farmers were taken from their farms to become soldiers. There were no more banquets at the palace. Footmen no longer carried out platters of pheasants roasted and decorated with their own tail feathers or mammoth sturgeons swimming in rich sauce. Though it broke Toma's heart, even our daily meals became simple, for the Empress said, "We must eat what our people are eating." We dined on cabbage soup, potatoes in sour cream, and pirozhki filled with bits of fish or hard-boiled egg.

When Olga turned up her nose at a dish of borsch, the Tsar said in a disapproving voice, "Shame on you, Olga. Think of what our brave soldiers are forced to get by on." I had never before heard him speak so harshly to one of the girls.

When winter came, we cut back on wood. Half the stoves in the palace remained cold. With all our sacrifices I could not help but think how comfortable we were. It was true some rooms were cold, but many were warm and cozy. Though pheasant and sturgeon were banished from the table, Toma saw to it that the cabbage soup had large chunks of tender meat.

The winter of 1914–15 was the coldest in years. The wounded soldiers who arrived at the Catherine Palace told stories of digging through the snow for a frozen carrot or turnip. Their fingers and toes were frostbitten. I asked myself why I should be warm and comfortable with a full belly when soldiers were suffering and dying. Even Stana no longer had easy answers.

"I wish Papa would find a way to end the war," she said. It was the closest she had ever come to questioning her father. She sighed. "Mama says we must pray harder, but I pray as hard as I can."

I prayed for Misha each night and thought of him all day long.

"Mama," I begged, "can't you ask the Tsar to find out where Misha is?"

"Katya, there are ten million Russian soldiers. Besides, think how much the Tsar has on his mind." Yet I saw that Mama was as worried about Misha as I was. She nursed the dying soldiers, afraid that at any moment she might see Misha on one of the stretchers.

When I read in the newspaper that nearly a million Russian soldiers had been taken prisoner, I kept awake at night trying to count to a million. I thought somehow that if I could count each prisoner, and Misha with them, the prisoners would be protected. Often I would stay awake into the early-morning hours, but I only got into the thousands—not enough.

The cold winter turned into a chilly spring and the spring into a rainy summer, the summer into a gloomy fall, and the news of the war was no better. One October morning, while we were having our simple breakfast of bread and tea and *tvorog,* with no jam to go with it, the Tsar announced, "I leave next week for army headquarters, and Alexei goes with me."

Alexei leaped up, shouting with pleasure.

The Empress uttered a sharp cry. Her eyes were blazing. She sprang from her chair. Grasping the dining table for support, she said, "You cannot think of taking Alexei to such a place. He is not well enough. Even if he were, we could not take such a step without consulting Father Grigory."

In the past the Tsar had given in to the Empress, especially in matters concerning Alexei, but now the Tsar thrust out his chin. In a firm voice he said, "Alexei is the heir to the throne, my dear. One day he will be Tsar. If he is to defend our country from its enemies, he must know what it is like to be a soldier. I'm afraid he has been coddled too much, for which I take full responsibility. I promise you, I will do whatever is necessary to see that he is well taken care of, but I have made up my mind."

We all sat with open mouths. The Empress was so taken aback by the Tsar's strong words that she could find no answer, but only sank down onto her chair and began to cry. Mama went to comfort her, but the Empress shook her off. She would not be comforted.

A week later the Tsar and Alexei left the palace for army headquarters.

CHAPTER EIGHT

RASPUTIN

Spring 1916–Winter 1917

The Empress fretted over Alexei all winter. She would
not rest until she saw for herself that he was well. The
Tsar wrote to discourage her, but nothing would
change her mind. In the spring arrangements were
made for a special train to take us to headquarters, a
journey of twenty-six hours. Several cars of the train
were hastily decorated. Rugs were laid down, and
comfortable chairs were arranged around delicate
tables. Besides the Grand Duchesses, Mama, and me,
accompanying us were footmen, cooks, the Empress's

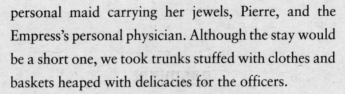

personal maid carrying her jewels, Pierre, and the Empress's personal physician. Although the stay would be a short one, we took trunks stuffed with clothes and baskets heaped with delicacies for the officers.

As we boarded the train, I saw hundreds of soldiers herded into empty railway cars with no furniture—just a layer of hay strewn over the floor. Like us, they were going to army headquarters, but unlike us, they would go on to the front. I was embarrassed at our show of luxury. I wondered what the soldiers thought of us as they watched us climb into our comfortable quarters, trailed by servants and piles of luggage.

I soon had my answer, for as news spread among the soldiers that the Empress would be traveling on their train, they looked toward us. When the Empress saw them and paused to raise her hand in greeting as she boarded, for once there was no return cheer. Though it was not talked of in the palace, only days before, I had read in one of the newspapers that there were no shells for the soldiers' rifles and no food for their stomachs. One Russian brigade had mutinied and killed their officer. I thought much had changed since the days when the crowds had cheered the imperial family in Palace Square. I wondered how we could win a war when our soldiers were so miserable.

At headquarters we lived in a world of men. Still, the men were sensible that the Empress and the Grand Duchesses were among them and that something must be done for them. Dinners were arranged. Trunks were opened and formal gowns, silk slippers, jewels, and furs were brought out. Slipping into dressy clothes in that busy military world made me feel like I was attending a masquerade.

I was fifteen now, and Stana was fourteen, so we were allowed to attend the dinners. The Tsar and his generals had brought silver serving pieces, fine china, and rare wines with them to headquarters. Soldiers had been sent out to hunt in the forest, and we dined well on grouse and venison. We might have been at a palace dinner, except for one thing. Several times during our dinner, officers appeared at the doorway of the dining salon looking anxious and embarrassed. They caught the eye of one general or another, and the general excused himself to read an urgent dispatch or give an order. Misha was out there somewhere, I thought. I could hardly force myself to choke down the elegant dinner, knowing soldiers might be dying as we banqueted.

As often as I could during our stay, I mentioned Misha's name in the hope that one of the officers might have heard of him. They smiled politely, but no one could tell me where he might be, or even recognized his name. Whenever I glimpsed an officer in the distance, I held my breath until he came close enough for me to see that it was not Misha. I tried to tell myself that Misha was safe, but nothing I heard at headquarters made me believe there was a safe place for a soldier. Even the Tsar appeared disheartened. When he was with his son, the Tsar beamed, but at other moments his shoulders sagged. He ran his hand over his beard and looked about him like a man who cannot escape a bloodthirsty beast.

However worried his father was, Alexei was in his glory. He was clearly the favorite of all the officers. He tugged at the Empress and his sisters, wanting to show them around headquarters and introduce them to his new friends. The men put their caps on his head and pretended to ask him for orders for this battle or that one. "He is our little general," they said, and patted him fondly. Each morning, while his father was having breakfast, Alexei stood guard outside the Tsar's tent, a small rifle on his shoulder. Only when the Tsar was finished would Alexei give up his guard duty. Even the Empress had to admit that Alexei was doing well.

At our farewell dinner, the night before we were to board our train to return to the palace, we tried to forget the war. There was a whole roast suckling pig commandeered from one of the nearby farms, caviar that had come in the Empress's hamper, and a towering cake, so tasty the cook was called in from the kitchen to take a bow. Olga, Tatiana, Marie, Stana, and I were surrounded with handsome, attentive officers. Even Mama flirted. A military band played waltzes during dinner. At the dinner's end there were gallant toasts to all the women present. In a strong voice one of the generals proposed a toast: "To the day when there will not be a single German soldier on Russian soil."

I applauded the toast, but it reminded me with a cruel stab how close the Germans were, and of the danger to Misha. I was ashamed of our extravagance and our gaiety. All the pleasure went from the evening.

Returning to the Alexander Palace, we found Anya waiting for us. She ran across the room to greet us and pressed a letter into Mama's hand. "It just came, Madame." There were tears in her eyes, for everyone knew that such envelopes from the army reported only bad news. Mama's hand trembled. She

handed the envelope to me. I had always turned to
Mama for comfort and strength, but now for the first
time in my life Mama was turning to me. I pulled her
to the sofa and sat down beside her. Anya shifted from
foot to foot like some small, fierce bird protecting its
nestlings. I tore the envelope open. The sound of the
tearing was like my heart being ripped apart. The
news was very bad, but it left us hope. The army
wished to inform us that Misha was a prisoner in
Germany. We were assured that the Russian army
would do all in its power to find him and return him
to his family.

When I told Stana, she put her arms around me
and kissed me and promised that her dear papa would
save Russia and bring home every prisoner of war, and
Misha would be the very first. I tried to find comfort
in her words, but I had heard the officers at army
headquarters say that the German soldiers were going
without food. I knew they would do what the starving

Russian soldiers were doing. They would feed their own army first. There would be little food left for prisoners.

That evening the Empress knocked softly at our door. In her hands she held her icon of St. Vladimir. "Stana told me about Misha, Irina. You must have this icon. Pray to St. Vladimir for Misha's safety. The saint will help you."

It was the icon the Empress valued most. I saw that Mama wanted to put her arms about the Empress in gratefulness and love, but she was afraid to be so forward. I was very glad I was not an empress but someone who could be hugged and comforted.

With the Tsar at the front, the Empress was relying more and more upon Rasputin. All summer and fall he came to the palace, swaggering down the halls and striding into the Empress's sitting room without so much as a by-your-leave. He acted as if he were in his own home, ordering the servants about and handling the delicate ornaments set out on the tables. It was terrible to see him pick up an exquisite vase in his clumsy hands with their dirty fingernails.

One evening, when the girls and I were gathered in Olga and Tatiana's room talking over the day, I asked, "How can your mama have such a person about?"

"You haven't seen Alexei suffering as we have," Tatiana said. "When he is ill, he cries all night long. His every move causes him terrible pain. Everything he suffers, Mama suffers twice as much. She has to listen to him plead, 'Mama, help me,' knowing there is nothing she can do. Rasputin makes him better. We don't know how. Mama thinks it is from God."

Under her breath Stana muttered darkly, "I think it is from the devil."

With the Tsar away, many of the decisions about the government were left to the Empress, whom the Tsar trusted completely. Our parliament, the Duma, had little power. They grumbled and made motions of governing, but the power was all the Tsar's, and he was far away. The Empress wrote to the Tsar daily, sometimes more often, to tell him what was happening in St. Petersburg, which was now officially called Petrograd, because "Petersburg" was German. Still, no one remembered to call it Petrograd, which had an ugly sound.

The Empress hated the Duma. She said there was no need for any government besides the Tsar. "We must be firm with the people," she said. "Russians love to feel the whip." I cringed to hear such cruel words. Misha, who was always in my thoughts, would have been very angry indeed.

Rasputin was on the Empress's side. They talked all day about ways to put an end to the Duma. Rasputin suggested appointing this minister and that one, men who were on his side, men so weak he could rule them. The Tsar, busy with the war and not wanting to anger the Empress, agreed with Rasputin's choices.

Stana confided to me that her uncles and aunt had

come to the Tsar and begged him to get rid of Rasputin. "They know how much the country hates him. But Papa always gives in to Mama."

The Empress and Rasputin were having their way, but the government was falling apart. Articles in the newspapers denounced Rasputin and the Empress as well. Suddenly everyone recalled that the Empress had once been a German princess, and they now accused her of being on the side of the Germans. Rasputin was said to be a German spy. The Duma was in an uproar. When we went out in public, people shook their fists at the Empress. She kept her chin high and looked straight ahead.

"Mama," I asked, "why doesn't the Empress let the people know that Alexei is ill and that Rasputin comes to the palace to help him?"

"The Empress and the Tsar don't want the people to know that Alexei is ill, Katya. One day Alexei may be the Tsar, and the people he rules should not believe him to be weak. A weak ruler would soon be overturned."

I could see what Mama meant, but the people continued to be so angry, I doubted that Alexei would ever have the chance to be Tsar.

It was in December, on one of Rasputin's frequent visits to the palace, that Stana and I caught him. We were sneaking down a back stairway to the dairy, for we knew it was the day for making farmer's cheese. One of the dairy maids, Nadya, would let us sample the cheese. With the Empress's new austerity, we were always hungry. As we neared the dairy room where the cream was separated from the milk, we heard a loud scuffling and angry voices. We stopped and looked at each other. It was not unusual to hear quarreling among the servants, but this had a different sound.

We tiptoed to the dairy doorway and peeked in. There was Rasputin, his strong arms around Nadya's waist, while she tried to squirm out of his grasp.

Rasputin was laughing at her struggles. "Now, my girl," he said, "if you keep on fighting me, you will soon be out of a job. The Empress has fired ministers of state for me; she will have no problem firing a maid."

Stana and I looked at each other. A moment later Stana marched into the dairy. I was right behind her. She announced to Rasputin, "I believe the Empress is looking for you. Shall I tell her that you are busy and can't come just now?"

Rasputin glared at Stana. There was so much hatred in his eyes, I was afraid he would strike her, but he only scuttled away. Nadya was sobbing. She threw her arms around Stana.

"That evil man will be back," she sobbed.

Stana said, "Don't worry, Nadya, we'll find a way to make sure that he leaves you alone."

We hurried away with the sound of Nadya's sobs still in our ears. When we were safely in our rooms, Stana asked, "What can I do?"

"Write a letter to your mama," I said. "I'll help you. Tell her exactly what we saw and heard. She'll believe her own daughter even if she doesn't believe anyone else. She knows you would never lie to her."

Together we wrote the letter:

My Dearest Mama,

It is only because I love you so much that I have to tell you a terrible thing. You must promise to believe me. Today in the dairy Katya and I saw Grigory Rasputin forcing dear Nadya to be his sweetheart even though she didn't want to and was struggling to get away. He said if she didn't do what he wanted, he would tell you she was a bad person and you would take away Nadya's job. Rasputin is very evil. I don't think he should come to the palace anymore.

Dear Mama, please believe me. Katya saw him too.

With God's blessing and all my love,
Your devoted daughter, Anastasia

We were a little frightened, but proud of our letter. For once someone would get the better of Rasputin. We planned to give the letter to the Empress right after tea, but we never did. A telegram came from the Tsar. Alexei was suffering from a nosebleed that could not be stopped. The Tsar was on his way home with Alexei. The Empress was so crushed, the telegram might have been a heavy club rather than a piece of paper. When she could speak, the Empress said, "Thank God Father Grigory is here."

That evening Alexei was carried into the palace on a stretcher. The nosebleed had not stopped. He was as white as a sheet of paper. His eyes had the beseeching look of a wounded animal. It was plain to see he was near death. The Empress pushed aside the Tsar and the stretcher bearers and threw her arms around Alexei. When at last she stood up, her silk gown was stained with his blood.

Rasputin strode into the room. "Let me see the boy, Mama," he said to the Empress. He stood gazing into Alexei's eyes for what seemed like hours but was only a few minutes. At last he turned to the Tsar and the Empress and said, "Don't be alarmed, Papa. Don't be alarmed, Mama. Nothing will happen." Moments later Alexei fell asleep. The bleeding had stopped.

Stana and I looked at each other. I saw her reach into her pocket and crumple the letter.

Everyone was hoping the Tsar would go to St. Petersburg and set the government to rights. The foolish and incompetent men chosen by Rasputin were destroying the country. Only that morning, when the people found there was no bread to buy, there had been riots in the streets. The soldiers ordered to stop the rioting refused to turn on the people. If there was no one to stop the riots, what would happen to the city?

But the Tsar would not go to St. Petersburg. "I must get back to my men," he said.

When we were alone, I asked, "Mama, how can the Tsar turn his back on St. Petersburg?"

Mama shook her head sadly. "It is true the Tsar wishes to be back with his armies, but he also wishes to be away from here with all the trouble in the Duma. If he leaves, the Empress and Rasputin will go on making difficulties. Now the Empress is talking of shutting down the Duma. And the trouble is not just in the city. I had a letter from Vitya at The Oaks. There are no men left in the village to do the work on the farm. They have all been conscripted into the army. Fifteen million men taken into the Russian army, our dear Misha taken prisoner, and for what?"

These were the first words I had heard Mama speak against the Empress. I could hardly believe my ears. I saw that Mama wished she had not spoken in front of me, but it was too late to take the words back.

"Perhaps I should not say such things, Katya, but you are sixteen now, and our future is with the future of the imperial family. If things go on as they are with such high-handedness, there will surely be a revolution."

I had never paid attention to Misha when he spoke

the terrible word "revolution." Now Mama was using it.

"But, Mama," I whispered, "in the French revolution the aristocracy all had their heads chopped off by the guillotine." We were members of the aristocracy.

Mama tried to smile. "Now, Katya, your imagination is running away with you. This is not France. You can be sure nothing will happen to the great families of Russia."

A week later, on a cold December day, the Empress learned that Rasputin was missing. At first we thought there was a plot by the people against the imperial family. That night we were all so frightened that Stana and her sisters and I all slept together in one room.

The next morning Rasputin's body was found in the Neva River. He was not murdered by the people but by an aristocrat and a relative of the Tsar. Prince Yussoupov, the richest man in Russia after the Tsar, and Grand Duke Dmitry, the Tsar's cousin, had murdered him! The terrible story came out bit by bit. The Prince and the Grand Duke had seen that all of Russia was furious because the crude and evil Rasputin was running their country. Over and over they had tried to tell this to the Tsar, but the Tsar would not listen. Fearing for the country, the two men invited Rasputin to the Prince's palace. They fed him poisoned petits fours. He ate them all up and did not die. They shot him. Still he did not die. Finally they hit him with a club and threw him into the river.

I could not get the image of the murdered man out of my mind. I had nightmares of his bloody body rising out of the icy Neva and making its way back to the palace.

The city of St. Petersburg rejoiced, but the Tsar was furious. The Prince was exiled to one of his estates in a far corner of Russia, and the Grand Duke was sent to Persia to fight in the army.

The Empress could not be consoled. After the funeral she wandered about the palace like a ghost, her eyes red and swollen from weeping. Mama and I took the icon of St. Vladimir to her and pressed it into her hands. She gave Mama so sad a look that Mama forgot all about her being the Empress and threw her arms around Alexandra.

When we were alone, I asked Mama, "Isn't the country better off without that evil man?"

Mama shook her head. "The country may be better off without him, Katya, but when it takes a murder to rescue a country, nothing will save it."

CHAPTER NINE

THE REVOLUTION

Winter 1917

There had never been a gloomier January. It was as if the sun had been exiled along with Rasputin's executioners. Snow never stopped falling from gray skies. I remembered my first year in the Alexander Palace and how we had skated and had snowball fights. Now we had lost the secret of enjoying ourselves.

The Tsar abandoned army headquarters and came to stay at the Alexander Palace. He followed the advances and retreats of the army, sticking paper flags on maps, but he showed little interest in the war.

When official dispatches were handed to him, he barely glanced at them. I sighed as I recalled Stana's promise that her father would bring Misha back. I was sorry for the Tsar, but I could not help being a little angry at his indifference.

The Tsar often wandered out by himself into the punishing weather, slogging through the snow for an hour at a time. He was always trailed at a discreet distance by a pair of armed Cossacks, for there were rumors of threats on the Tsar's life. The scarlet jackets of the Cossacks were the only bright spots in the gloomy landscape. In the evenings the Tsar sat silently pasting the hundreds of photographs he had taken of the imperial family into albums, as if he wanted to preserve memories of happier times.

The Empress did not even try to play her sad music on the piano. The busy hands that had always held some embroidery as an example to the girls now lay idle upon her lap. She seldom went to the Catherine Palace to nurse the soldiers. The girls tried to cheer her, taking turns spending the day at her side.

The only thing that interested her was the coming and going of the government ministers. When they met with the Tsar in his study, she asked that he leave the door ajar so that she might listen to their reports. When they left, she hurried to consult with the Tsar. She could be heard denouncing any minister who expressed a wish for a democratic government.

The Empress's response to such talk was "Don't listen to such nonsense. You are the Tsar of all the Russias. We must pass on a strong monarchy to Alexei."

Stana and I still visited the soldiers. As I talked with them, I prayed that they would bring me some word of Misha. France and England were at last sending arms to Russia. With the new arms the Russian army was able to retake German land it had once given up. As the Germans retreated, they were releasing Russian prisoners of war.

Each day I eagerly looked through the hospital

admission records and examined the faces of the soldiers who were brought in. I questioned them to find out if they had heard of Misha, showing his picture to any soldier who would look at it. No one had seen him. The soldiers shook their heads and said, "I'm sorry, Miss; I wish I could help you."

Stana tried to comfort me. "Don't you worry. He'll turn up," she said. I tried to believe her.

Stana was with me when it happened. All morning she and I had labored with Pierre over French verbs. We were not planning to go to the hospital. Anya had promised to show Stana and me how to pin our long hair up properly. "If you attend a formal occasion, you must look like the young ladies you are." But at the last moment Mama had a headache, and Anya sent us off. "Go and amuse yourselves. I must see to Madame."

With nothing to do, and the palace so gloomy, we begged a ride to the hospital. Cheering the soldiers always cheered us as well. One of the officers was looking for us. "Well, Miss Katya, and the Grand

Duchess, too, we were just about to send a message to the palace. Someone wants to see you."

From the pleased expression on the his face, I guessed that it was Misha. "Where! Where!" I cried. Without even waiting for an answer, I began to run through the ward, searching for Misha. A man on crutches walked toward me, a smile on his face. He was thin, with a shaven head, hollow cheeks, and sunken eyes. He appeared half starved. Impatiently I looked past him, searching for Misha.

"Katya," the man said, "aren't you going to say hello? I've come a long way to see you."

I knew the voice. I looked into Misha's eyes. Sobbing, I threw my arms around him with such force that his crutches fell to the floor, and I had to support him until we could get untangled.

"Have pity on me, Katya. Your assault is worse than having the whole German army against me."

"Misha, where did you come from? Why are you on crutches? Oh, Misha, I thought I would never see you again. St. Vladimir must have brought you back."

"So that was St. Vladimir driving a wagon pulled by a lame horse? I thought it was a peasant hoping to make a few rubles by selling me back to the Russian army."

The whole ward was staring at us. Several of the men were laughing. "Katya," Misha said, "you know this place. Surely there is a corner where we can talk. And where are your manners? Introduce me to your young friend."

I had completely forgotten Stana. "This is Grand Duchess Anastasia Nikolayevna," I said. "Stana, this is Mikhail Sergeyevich Gnedich."

Misha gave the best formal bow he could, considering his crutches. Stana cheerfully shook his hand and declared that she was pleased to see him safe. Then, glancing from one of us to the other, she quickly said, "I promised to play chess with one of the soldiers." She began to giggle.

Hastily I led Misha away to a small room where

supplies were kept. Pushing aside washbasins and towels, we sat down on a bench. I was still holding on to him. I felt if I let go, he would disappear again.

"Misha," I said, noticing for the first time a gold medal pinned to his chest, "you have been awarded the George Cross! That means you have been in great danger. You must tell me what happened to you. We only knew that you were a prisoner."

"There isn't much to tell." His voice was strained and hoarse. "The Germans encircled our regiment. Half of our men were killed, and the rest of us were marched into German territory. When the Germans were short of horses, they hitched prisoners up to move their artillery wagons. Some of us would not move cannons into a position to bombard our own men. The Germans started shooting those who refused. I thought I would be next, but an officer said, 'Let the rest be. We need men to cut wood.'

"We worked in the forest from sunup to sundown. In the summer it wasn't so bad. We foraged in the woods for the shoots of young ferns. There were ponds where we could dig in the muck for the roots of water lilies." Misha grimaced. "It was all very tasty. Then winter came down upon us. Our boots wore out, and we wrapped our feet in rags. Snow was our water and the bark of trees our food. Every few days we were given a little porridge. When the Russian army began to take back what the Germans had seized, the Germans fled, leaving us behind. That's when I hitched a ride with St. Vladimir and his lame horse.

"And I am a little lame myself," he added. "While I was cutting wood, a tree trunk fell on my leg." When he saw the expression on my face, he quickly reassured me. "It is nothing. They've bandaged it up, and the doctor told me to stay off it for a few days."

He took my hands in his and smiled. "The soldiers here tell me that you and Aunt Irina and the Grand Duchesses and even the Empress have become nurses." He gave me a serious look. "I have heard nothing but good of you, Katya. *Molodyets!* Well done!" He continued to look closely at me until I felt my face flush. His voice became tender. "You are sixteen, now, Katya. A young lady. Who would have thought it?"

My heart turned over at his words. I felt my cheeks burning.

He smiled. "Now, Katya, you have heard my story. Let me hear yours. How is Aunt Irina, and what have you been up to?" He gave me one of the tolerant smiles he had sent my way when I was a child, but his words were bitter. "I suppose life is very merry at the Alexander Palace."

I was so happy to see him, I forgave him his condescension. "Oh, Misha," I said in a low voice, anxious to at last have someone to confide in, "things could not be worse. The Empress is terribly sad because Rasputin was murdered, so there is no one to help Alexei, and the Tsar is like a man asleep. He spends all his time pasting pictures into an album."

I heard a cry and, looking around, saw Mama. She

threw her arms around Misha. "Anastasia hurried to tell me, and I flew over here. Misha, you are so thin. And your poor leg! You must tell me everything."

After Misha had repeated his story to Mama, she took his hand and said, "The Empress has been most thoughtful. She has invited you to stay in the palace until you are better."

Misha's face tightened. "I am sure she means well, but I will never accept the Tsar's hospitality."

I was not surprised. I even admired Misha's independence a little, but Mama was hurt. "Misha, you must believe the Tsar means nothing but kindness."

"Forgive me, Aunt Irina. I am sure the invitation was kindly meant, but if you had seen, as I have, what this war of the Tsar's is costing our country, you would feel the same. He threw fifteen million men into the war. Half of them are wounded or prisoners—or dead. The Tsar doesn't want for food, but the villagers in the countryside are starving. There are no crops, for the peasants are all fighting Germans, and what little remains is commandeered by an army desperate for food. And Katya tells me the Tsar spends his time gluing photographs into an album. I'll tell you this: If there is a revolution, the army will not come to the Tsar's aid. The men cannot forgive him. No! I'll die before I spend one night under the Tsar's roof."

Misha's face was feverish, and his eyes were like two points of fire. In the past Mama would have been indignant at such words, but now, seeing how sick he was, she did not argue with him but only said, "I'll ask if we can't take you to St. Petersburg for a few weeks until you are yourself again. But Misha"—Mama looked about—"you must guard your tongue. It is not safe to say such things in front of other people."

Misha nodded. "Of course, I promise. You are right, Aunt Irina; I am still recovering. No doubt I will come to my senses." I knew that Misha was sparing Mama. I also knew he believed every word of what he had said. His words made me think of Alexei's war game, with its little cardboard cannons and hospital wagons, and how at the time we had taken pleasure in its cleverness, not understanding how cruel the real game of war was.

A week later, when Misha was well enough to leave the hospital, Mama and I took him home to St. Petersburg and the Zhukovsky mansion. I tried to pretend being back there with Misha was like the old days, but it wasn't. Misha had changed. He still teased me, but there was a hard edge to his humor. Often, when he wasn't aware of my watching him, I saw a look of panic on his face, as if he feared that at any moment the German army would march through our door and drag him away.

It was only when he took to wandering the city streets and searching out the few friends of his who were not missing in the war that he began to take an interest in life once again.

For myself, I had been away from St. Petersburg for so long that I was amazed to see what was going on there. Though it was one of the coldest Februarys on record, people milled about in the streets. With the miners in the army, there wasn't enough coal to run the factories, so thousands were without work. Students gathered in angry knots, shouting slogans and waving red flags.

As long as Mama was in the room, Misha said nothing about all of this, but when the two of us were alone, he was too excited to keep still. His proudest moment came when his hero, Alexander Kerensky, stood up in the Duma and actually called for the Tsar's abdication. "He is the only leader with courage," Misha said. "The Tsar would do well to listen to him. With Kerensky there is still a chance for a democratic government. Without him, it will be Lenin and Stalin, and Russia will be finished."

Kerensky didn't go to jail. Instead, all across the city, people supported him, calling for the Tsar to step down. I did not know what to think. Certainly the Tsar had led his people into a terrible war and had abandoned his responsibilities, but I would not be happy to see the country in the hands of some of the revolutionaries I had seen on the streets.

Misha had secrets he would not share, and kept his thoughts to himself. He could walk now without his crutches. His face filled out, and his hair grew back into tight curls he could not smooth. In the mornings he sat reading the papers or stood at the window watching the crowds on the Nevsky. In the afternoons he went out, saying only that he wanted to get a bit of air. When I asked to go along, he said, "The streets have become too dangerous, Katya." I guessed that he was meeting his revolutionary friends, for when he returned from his walks, his eyes were bright and he walked with a brisker step. The look of panic had disappeared. Often I saw leaflets tucked into his pockets.

The winter would not stop. In the Summer Garden the statues were hidden under a blanket of white. The snow, which in the past had seemed so beautiful and pure to me, now felt as if it were pressing down upon the city, crushing it with its light weight. People were stealing benches from the park and breaking them up for wood. The Neva was still frozen, and what little wood came into the city came on sleighs and was so expensive that only the very rich could afford it. The rooms of our mansion were never really warm. We wore sweaters over our clothes and slept under two feather quilts.

Mama wrote cheerful letters daily to the Empress, never mentioning the angry crowds in the city. Instead she sent bits of gossip about friends—for incredibly, in the palaces and mansions parties were still going on. I enclosed notes to Stana finding fault with the weather and asking what studies with Pierre I was missing. In her notes to me she spoke of Alexei being ill and complained that without me there was no one with whom to have a bit of fun. She hoped I would soon be back.

One afternoon, when I complained for the hundredth time that I was bored, Misha took pity on me.

"Come, I'll take you to a café for a cup of chocolate

and cakes, though we will be lucky to get weak tea and a thin slice of bread."

In spite of the freezing weather, I felt quite happy as we started out. I was wearing my favorite coat with its collar and hem trimmed in fur, a matching fur hat pulled down over my ears. My hand, snug in its mitten, was tucked into Misha's arm. As we passed Palace Square, we both looked up at the angel. It was still there. Saying nothing, we looked at each other and smiled.

My pleasure in the outing soon disappeared. Many of the buildings had hand-lettered banners calling for revolution and demanding an end to the war. I too would have been happy to see an end of the war, but I was shocked to see posters with a picture of the Empress and, underneath, the old accusation that she was a spy for the Germans. I complained to Misha, "No one loves Russia or wishes more for a Russian victory over the Germans than the Empress."

Misha said, "It's hunger and frustration with the

war that makes the people lash out like that."

"But it's so unfair," I insisted.

"It's one unfair thing among many," Misha answered.

In front of a bakery, we skirted a line that stretched for several blocks. The faces of the women waiting for bread were red with cold. They hopped from one foot to the other and beat their arms against their chests to keep warm. Their envious glances at my warm coat made me uncomfortable.

"Bread has gone from four kopecks to seven kopecks a pound," Misha said. "Where are those women to get such money?" A sign went up in the window of the bakery: NO MORE BREAD. Immediately there were shouts of anger and the sound of glass breaking. As the angry women surged into the bakery, Misha hurried me across the prospekt. Safely on the other side, we watched the women carrying out bags of flour. Policemen stood by, joking with the women.

"The police aren't arresting the women," I said.

Misha shrugged. "The policemen are as hungry as they are. They will never arrest them."

When we reached the café, there was, as Misha had suspected, nothing to be had but weak tea. There wasn't even thin-sliced bread. Still, there was bread for us at home. That could not be right. I hated the war that brought only death and starvation. Now I saw that the Tsar was truly in danger and that a revolution might take place. How different conditions in the outside world seemed from the safety of the palace. I wondered what the Tsar and the Empress would think if they could walk the streets of St. Petersburg.

We had been in the café only a short time when two men, like Misha in their early twenties, came over to our table and gave me a questioning look.

"Sit down," Misha said. "This is only my cousin. She won't do us any harm." He didn't introduce me to his friends. I guessed he did not want me to know their names.

One of the men had a flat-visored cap and a scarf

wound around and around his neck as if he were nursing a sore throat. The other man had long black hair hanging down in greasy wisps from under a fur hat. The man with the scarf said, "There's going to be a general *zabastovka* tomorrow. Everyone is talking about it. The students are going out. The workers will leave their factories. Even the trolleys will stop running."

The long-haired man said in a low voice, "We are hoping some of the army will join the strike."

"At least," Misha said, "the army will not shoot the demonstrators."

The next day Misha was proven wrong. The Tsar, furious that the city should be shut down by a strike in a time of war, forbade all public meetings and ordered the strikers to go back to work or be drafted into the army.

For a day the strikers obeyed, and the city was quiet. Mama and I stood at the windows looking out on the Nevsky, where only a handful of people could be seen. The following day the strikers were out on the streets once more. Misha left early in the morning. When Mama pleaded with him to remain at home, he only shook his head.

"Aunt Irina, it is to your benefit to have someone who knows what is going on in the city. The time may come when you will be in danger."

"That's nonsense. You are playing at revolution as if it were a game, but Misha, it is a dangerous game, and you must keep clear of Kerensky and his people."

When Misha returned home, he was furious. "A stupid army officer ordered his men to fire on the demonstrators. Fifty strikers lie dead. But not all the army obeyed the Tsar. One regiment refused to shoot the strikers. Instead they killed the officer who had given them the order! The Tsar must abdicate, or the whole country will be in turmoil."

Mama listened to Misha with growing alarm. "Surely this chaos can't go on. The country must come to its senses and settle down." Mama still hoped all would come right. How could that be? How could the

country settle down, with millions of soldiers dead
and the whole country starving?

Looking out the window the next day, we saw soldiers, each with the red flag of the revolution hanging
from his bayonet. We could see smoke from burning
buildings. Misha burst into the house. Without stopping to take a breath, he blurted out, "The arsenal
where weapons are stored has been emptied, and the
law courts are burning. The revolutionaries have
released prisoners from jail. They've taken over the
Winter Palace and arrested the Tsar's ministers.
Kerensky has formed a revolutionary government."

Misha paused to catch his breath. He looked at us
as if he didn't know whether to continue. This time he
spoke in a quiet voice. "The Tsar has abdicated."

I was too shocked to say a word.

"I don't believe it," Mama said. "The Tsar would
never abdicate."

"I assure you, Aunt Irina, it's true."

After a long moment Mama said, "I must return

to the Alexander Palace at once. The Empress will need me."

Misha said, "I beg you not to go, Aunt Irina. It won't be safe there."

"What do you mean, Misha?" she said. "What place could be safer than the Tsar's palace? It is surrounded by loyal guards."

Misha warned, "When they see which way the wind is blowing, how long will the guards remain loyal? I tell you, if you join the imperial family, your life will be in danger."

Mama squared her shoulders. "At any rate *I* will be loyal."

"I'm going with you, Mama." I believed Misha. If the soldiers were supporting a revolution, what hope was there that the guard would protect the Tsar and his family? The Tsar and the Empress were like family to me. Stana and her sisters were like my sisters. If there was to be a revolution, I would stand by them.

"I won't let you come, Katya," Mama said. "You heard Misha. It's too dangerous."

"I heard you, too, Mama. I can be loyal as well."

Mama gave me a long look, as if she were seeing something she had not seen before. At last she nodded slowly. "Very well. We must get ready at once."

We planned to leave the next morning, but that evening Misha, who had returned to the streets, hurried into our rooms, where we were still packing.

"Mobs are breaking into the mansions of the rich and looting and burning," he said. "Some of us tried to stop them, but they are crazy with power. They will be here next."

Misha ordered us to lock the doors and close the draperies. He searched frantically for pen and paper. With a shaking hand he printed: KEEP OUT. THIS HOUSE IS THE PROPERTY OF THE REVOLUTIONARY GOVERNMENT. He tacked the sign on the front door.

From behind our closed draperies we could hear a

mob approaching. There were shouts and curses. We held our breath. The shouting faded. The crowd moved on.

Mama was grateful to Misha, but I was full of anger. I had come to believe the war was a disaster. I had seen the women fighting for a bit of bread, but this was as bad. Furious, I said, "Those are your revolutionaries. They are nothing more than a mob, stealing and burning." I expected Misha to turn on me. Instead he was silent, a look of misery on his face.

At last in a low voice he said, "Those are not *my* revolutionaries, Katya. Once a revolution gets under way, it attracts evil men as well as good men. Now you had better finish your packing. I'll find a car for you." He looked at us for a moment. "I would rather not say this, but I must be honest. The mansion is protected for now, but tomorrow may be different. Take the things you value most with you."

Mama gathered her jewels, her favorite icons, and Papa's portrait. I took my diary and the gold locket in the shape of a four-leaf clover with the portraits of the Grand Duchesses. When we were ready to leave, our small suitcases seemed very little to carry out of so large a home.

Once Mama had employed fifty servants. Now there were only a handful. We smothered Anya with kisses. Mama paid each of the remaining servants a month's wages, and we bade everyone good-bye. We looked about us one last time and then hurried out through a back door. Misha handed us into the car he had arranged for us to ride in. As we kissed him good-bye, Mama asked, "What will you do, Misha?"

"I've waited a long time for this day. I'll support the revolution and Kerensky's government. But I will pray for you—and if Lenin takes over, I will pray for the Tsar and his family, for they will need my prayers."

As the car drove off, I looked over my shoulder. Misha had already turned away.

CHAPTER TEN

LAST DAYS AT THE ALEXANDER PALACE

Winter–Summer 1917

It was late evening when we reached the gates of the Alexander Palace. A March fog hovered over patches of snow, making the palace grounds seem nothing more than a blur. There were no Imperial Guard or scarlet-jacketed Cossacks. There were soldiers with angry, sullen faces. "You can't go in there," one of the soldiers snarled at us. "No one is allowed in or out." He looked at our suitcases with suspicion.

"I am the Empress's lady-in-waiting," Mama said.

"There is no Empress in there; there is only the

German spy." The soldier gave a nasty laugh. "There is no more Tsar. There is only Mr. Colonel."

His words sent a chill down my spine. The world was turned upside down. I began to understand our own danger. An officer strolled over. His questions were more polite, but his manner was just as cold. At last he agreed to allow us to enter the palace. "But first we must see what is in your suitcases."

With the smirking soldiers looking on and to our great embarrassment, the officer rummaged through our dresses and petticoats. When he came to Mama's jewelry box, he said, "How do I know these jewels are not stolen?"

Mama was furious. "Do I look like a thief?"

"All you nobles are thieves! These must be turned over to the people's government. I know you aristocrats. You will sell the jewels and send the money to those who are fighting against the revolution."

Mama was about to protest, but the hostile looks on the faces of the soldiers frightened her. Later she told the Empress, "All I could think of was getting myself and Katya safely inside the palace and away from those beasts. I was terrified that we would be arrested and taken away. If the jewels were our ransom, so be it."

The Empress was as white and rigid as a marble statue. She had never looked more regal. "How terrible that I have caused you this trouble, Irina. You were very good to come to me. And you too, dear Katya. We are a sad family. Nothing can be done until the Tsar arrives. He was visiting the troops at the front, and his returning train was stopped by a mob of evil soldiers. Irina, I cannot believe that Nikolai has abdicated. What will become of us, and what will become of poor Russia?"

Mama looked about. "Where are the girls and Alexei? They are safe?"

"Yes, safe, but very ill. They have all come down with measles. We nearly lost Marie. What of Katya?

Has she had measles? If not, she had better keep away from them."

"I've had measles, Madame," I said, remembering very well the itchy rash and the headache that felt like a trapped bird was beating its wings in my head.

"Well, then, run in and see them, Katya. They need cheering."

The girls were spotted and red-eyed. Stana said, "We're all going to have our heads shaved tomorrow."

I couldn't believe my ears. "Why?"

"The measles has made some of our hair fall out, and Mama says it will grow back faster if we shave it all off."

I looked at Marie's long golden curls and the older girls' elegant coiffures.

"We hate it," Marie said, "but Mama is so upset, we don't want to argue with her. She has much to worry her."

Their father was no longer Tsar, they were prisoners

in their own palace, and now they had to have their heads shaved. "I'm going to get mine shaved too," I announced.

"Why?" Stana asked. "You don't have measles."

"I don't care. We'll do it together."

They looked at me for a moment, and then we all burst out laughing.

When the palace barber came the next day, I had second thoughts, but the girls were so brave as their locks fell to the floor, I could not be less brave. When it was over, we stared at one another, hardly recognizing ourselves. We tried to laugh, but it was harder this time.

No sooner had Mama and I settled into our places in the palace than we heard that drunken soldiers were looting the stores in the village and drinking up all the wine and liquor they could steal. They were cursing the Tsar and the Empress and threatening to break into the palace. As darkness fell, soldiers milled about the gates shouting, "Down with the Tsar! Down with the Empress!" With horror we realized they were the very regiment of soldiers meant to protect the palace. Misha had been right. Except for the palace guard, we were now left undefended.

When she realized the soldiers had deserted us, the Empress hastily threw a cloak over her shoulders and went out to the palace guard. Stana and Marie and I went with her. She went from soldier to soldier, greeting each and imploring him to be loyal to the Tsar. "You are all that stands between my children and the gravest danger," the Empress said. "Our lives are in your hands. I know we can trust you." She made the sign of the cross over them, and they in turn kissed her hand. At last we returned through the darkness into the palace, but none of us slept that night.

The government, now led by Kerensky, sent a new regiment of soldiers to guard the palace, but nothing in their hostile manner reassured us. "If only your dear papa were here," the Empress kept saying to the girls, but one day passed and a second. We had nearly given up hope, fearing that the Tsar had been arrested and taken to Moscow, when we heard a commotion at the gate of the palace. The Empress called out joyfully, "Alexei! Girls! It's your papa!" It was true. There at the gate of the palace was the Tsar.

The soldiers stopped him. "This is outrageous!" the Empress said. "They are keeping the Tsar from entering his own palace." I believed that but for Mama's calming words, the Empress would have rushed out and attacked the guards. At last the gates were opened, and a moment later the girls rushed into their papa's arms.

The Tsar, with his arms around the girls, exclaimed, "My little fledglings. You look like plucked birds." He looked up at Mama and me. "Irina, Katya, I am so grateful to you for coming at this time. Now that I am with my beloved family, nothing else matters."

Indeed, the Tsar did look as though a burden had fallen away. His carriage was more upright, his face had more color, and his step was brisker than when I had last seen him. It was almost as if once the terrible step of abdication had been taken, there was nothing he could not face.

The Empress spoke of the abdication immediately. "How could you have done it, Nicky? They must have forced you. The country is surely still behind you."

"No, my dear, it is not. There is mutiny in the army." He paused, and his face took on a look of great sadness. "My own generals sent me a letter begging me to abdicate. That decided me." He bowed his head. "I pleaded with them to allow me to enlist in the army as a plain soldier. 'If I cannot rule Russia, at least let me fight for her,' I said. But they refused me even that."

The Empress asked, "But then is Alexei to be the Tsar?"

"At first that's what I asked, but they pointed out to me that our family would probably be exiled from Russia. If Alexei were Tsar, we would have to leave him behind. Who would care for him as you have, my dear? It could not be done. He would be ill in no time."

"Then who?" The Empress thought for a moment and said, "Your younger brother, Mikhail."

"Yes. I named Mikhail, but he refused."

The Empress was shocked. "He would not become the Tsar! How can that be? The greatest honor in the world."

The Tsar took her hand. "My dear, the world has changed. There is much danger and no honor in being the Tsar. Our country has decided it can do without one."

After that we heard no more about the abdication. What might have been said in private between the Tsar and the Empress we could only guess.

The telephone was taken away from us, and all letters going out or coming in were censored. We found the soldiers' dirty fingerprints on the heavy cream-colored stationery of the Tsar's mother and the Empress's sister.

Many of the palace staff, once numbering hundreds, were dismissed. Instead of impeccably uniformed footmen treading silently along the corridors, we saw rowdy soldiers, their caps askew, their shirts hanging over their pants. They tramped up and down the hallways, poking into our rooms and watching our every move. We even caught one of them stealing a bracelet from Olga's room. We didn't dare complain, for we would have been accused of suggesting that a member of the revolutionary army was dishonest. For that we might have been sent off to prison.

Until her father told her to stop, Stana made faces behind the soldiers' backs. "They are not part of some game, my dear," the Tsar said. "Whatever their faults, our lives depend upon them."

We learned that was true one evening, when we heard the sound of shots. We ran to the windows. Below us were hundreds of angry demonstrators. The unruly mob had marched all the way from St. Petersburg to take revenge on the Tsar and the Empress. Their clumsily lettered signs read DEATH TO THE TSAR and EXECUTE THE GERMAN SPY. The Tsar took one look and then strode hastily to his room, coming back with his regimental sword drawn. He held the sword so tightly, we could see the blood drain from his fingers.

The mob pushed against the gates. The soldiers guarding the palace leveled their guns. Instead of our tormentors, the soldiers became our protectors. At first the mob could not believe that the soldiers would fire on them. When bullets exploded over their heads in a warning, the mob drew back. For two hours they stood outside the gates, screaming insults at the royal family and taunting the soldiers. At last they turned back toward St. Petersburg.

The Tsar went out at once to thank the soldiers. Instead of accepting the Tsar's gratitude, they angrily confiscated his sword.

Our days of imprisonment dragged on. Pierre remained with us to teach us French and literature and to care for Alexei. His once-soft face had hardened. He no longer read us romantic poems. Instead he told us stories of brave heroes who showed great courage.

The Tsar himself took over the teaching of geography. He was an excellent instructor, patient and thorough. For every country we studied he had a story. As a young man the Tsar had been sent all over the world. He had killed tigers in India and climbed the pyramids in Egypt. He had met the King of Siam and nearly been killed in Japan by a samurai's sword. The Tsar showed us the scar on his forehead. When we looked at the map he spread out before us, we did not see flat bits of different colors but whole countries full of exciting adventure.

We were enchanted by the stories he told us. We saw the pleasure the telling gave him, for in the stories he was not a deposed and imprisoned man but a young tsarevich traveling all over the world on imperial yachts and elegant trains, welcomed by kings and queens.

The Easter of 1917 was a chilly one, with snowflakes still swirling about. Stana and I begged onion skins and beets from Toma so that we could dye

Easter eggs. Only a few eggs could be spared. Because they were precious, we took pains with our efforts, carefully stenciling in wax all of our names. When the eggs were dipped into the dye, the name stood out in white. On her papa's egg Stana had written "Tsar Nikolai II."

Under heavy guard we were allowed to visit the Cathedral of St. Catherine for the Easter vigil. The service went on for many hours, but it was not too long for us, for we were delighted to be free of our palace prison. At the end of the service everyone received a candle for the traditional procession around the church celebrating the moment of Christ's resurrection. I looked forward to the procession, for the sight of all those small tongues of flame flickering in the darkness of the Russian night never ceased to thrill me.

It was not to be. The soldiers said it would cause trouble if we took part in the procession, and they sent all of us, like bad children, off to the palace. Watching the disappointed Tsar give in to his tormentors, his step heavy, his head down, I thought of our last Easter together, when the Tsar had fulfilled his Easter duty by planting a kiss on the cheek of each and every one of the thousand soldiers in his regiment. It had taken him the whole of Easter Sunday. And how they had cheered him!

Things improved the moment we stepped into the palace. "I smell *kulich*," Alexei cried, and ran toward the dining room. There it was, like a golden crown, a rich Easter cake. Toma was hovering at the door to see our response. Alexei ran to her and threw his arms around her.

When she could catch her breath, she announced, "All during Lent when we were fasting, I hoarded the eggs and butter. It took two dozen eggs and only the good Lord knows how much butter to make this cake. Now sit down and enjoy the feast."

I saw how pleased she was to see happy smiles for once. There were platters of ham with horseradish sauce, kasha, and sauerkraut, and a beautiful *paskha*, so smooth and sweet, it slid down our throats. After dinner we broke the eggs we had dyed and gave one another warm kisses. One person would exclaim, "*Khristos voskres*; Christ has risen," to which another person would respond in turn, "*Voistinu voskres*; indeed, He has risen!"

Though we protested, the Tsar took some slices of *kulich* and *paskha* down to the guards. I heard him say, "Christ has risen," and I heard the guards respond, "Indeed, He has risen!"

The next day the Tsar called us together. With something of his old regal bearing he announced, "I have just learned that the Minister of Justice, Alexander Kerensky, will visit us today."

"That brute!" the Empress said. "He is the one who has imprisoned us."

The Tsar took her hand. "My dear, I understand how you feel, but that is just the response that we must guard against. Kerensky is the leader of the revolutionary government in Russia. The whole country does his bidding. For the sake of Russia we must do everything we can to make his job easier, and Sunny, we need him on our side."

The Empress was indignant, but his pet name for her helped to calm her. "But why, Nicky, why should we lift a finger to help him?"

"There are two reasons. First of all I believe he means us no harm. We have been imprisoned for our own protection. Second, the Bolsheviks are breathing down Kerensky's neck. If the Bolshevik leader, Lenin, takes over the government, then, my dear, we are all finished and Russia as well."

His solemn words impressed even the Empress, and we all resolved to be on our good behavior, but we were frightened of our meeting with this man, who held our fate and the fate of Russia in his hands.

The moment I heard the Tsar say his name, I remembered how Misha looked up to Kerensky. That made me feel a little better. There had been nothing more than the briefest notes from Misha. To Mama he said only that he was well and keeping out of trouble. To me he wrote that he was devoting his time to organizing the university students into a revolutionary committee. I didn't dare to share his letters with Stana, for the girls were loyal to their father and hated the revolution with all their hearts.

We knew at once when Kerensky arrived at the palace. The soldiers' caps were slapped on their heads, their shirts tucked into trousers, and their tunics straightened. As we waited, a servant whispered to us that Kerensky was having all our rooms searched. There was fire in the Empress's eyes.

At last the double doors to the sitting room swung open. I don't know what I expected, perhaps a great bear of a man all dressed in revolutionary red. Instead, a very normal-sized man, in his mid-thirties, looking like a schoolmaster, walked into the room. He was severe and formal and appeared very uncomfortable, running his hand through his hair, which was cut short like the bristles on a brush. After a moment's hesitation he shook the Tsar's outstretched hand and acknowledged each of us with a stiff bow. He made a little polite conversation.

"You are comfortable here? Well cared for?" he asked.

The Tsar said, "Very comfortable, thank you."

I could see that it was all the Empress could do to follow her husband's instructions, for she looked as if she longed to pick up a vase and hit Mr. Kerensky over the head.

As Kerensky left, he said, "I regret that I must return to carry on an investigation that will take some little time."

The investigation began the following week, and it centered around the Empress and the accusations against her as a German spy. The Tsar and the Empress were separated and repeatedly questioned. The palace was even searched for a wireless radio that the Empress might be using to send secret messages to Germany!

For weeks the Tsar and the Empress were forbidden to speak to each other. "If you disobey this rule," Kerensky told them, "we will have to send the Empress away." We all knew that meant prison. The Tsar and the Empress spoke not a word, though their eyes never left each other's face.

The investigation went on and on. The Tsar, who would willingly have borne any insults against himself, found it hard to keep his temper when the Empress was under suspicion. At first Kerensky was hostile toward both of them, but as he spent more time at the palace, his behavior toward the Tsar and the Empress grew kinder. I thought he might be seeing them as a frightened mother and father, living a simple life, tender with their children and courteous to everyone from the highest to the lowest on the palace staff.

Alexei was having more nosebleeds, and the Empress was always at his side. Kerensky must have found it difficult to believe the dignified woman who so gently nursed her ill son could be the German spy pictured in cartoons as bathing in the blood of revolutionaries. At last he gave up the investigation and dismissed all charges of treason. Kerensky said to the Tsar, "Sir, your wife does not lie."

To which the Tsar replied, "That, sir, is something I have always known."

Kerensky continued his visits to the palace. One day, while we were all having tea together, Kerensky brought us bad news. He did not even wait to take the Tsar aside, but in front of all of us he announced that Lenin had returned from exile. "He's in St. Petersburg, leading the Bolsheviks in demonstrations against our new government and against the war as well. The man is nothing but trouble."

The Tsar was disgusted. "An end to the war would mean a surrender to Germany. The Germans will divide Russia like a birthday cake."

Kerensky said, "The Germans know that. It was

the Germans who sent Lenin back here. He came in one of their trains. He owes them much for that, but as long as I am in charge, we will never give in to the Germans."

Speaking in a low voice, Kerensky said to the Tsar, "I must tell you that I have abolished the death penalty."

"But that is absolute foolishness," the Tsar said. "If you cannot put deserting soldiers and dangerous criminals to death, there will be chaos in the army and looting in the streets."

Kerensky nibbled at his lower lip. In an even quieter voice he said, "I did it not for the deserters and the criminals, sir, but for you."

Angrily the Tsar replied, "If you have abolished the death penalty to save my life, let me tell you there was no need. I am ready to give my life for the good of my country."

After Kerensky left us, we looked at one another

and were silent. The Empress was pale. The Tsar took her hand. It was several moments before any of us could speak.

In his past visits, Kerensky had reassured the imperial family that plans were under way for them to leave Russia for England, where the Tsar's cousin, King George V, would take them in, but this time he had said nothing of England. We began to give up hope of an escape.

A few days later I happened to be near a room where Kerensky sat alone going over some papers. I lingered for a moment at the door, trying to get up my courage to speak with him. Kerensky looked up and smiled at me. When he saw the expression on my face, he said, "Is there something you want?"

"Please, sir," I said, my voice cracking with nervousness, "I have a cousin, Mikhail Sergeyevich Gnedich, who is a revolutionary. I wonder if you know him. He often speaks of you."

Kerensky smiled. "I'm afraid I don't know the lad. There are many young men at the university who support us. Perhaps he is one of them. I will seek him out." He smiled. "And are you a revolutionary?"

"I have seen much suffering in Russia," I said. "I know there must be changes, but the imperial family are like my own."

A sad smile came over Kerensky's face. "Loyalty is a good thing. I wish I had more of it among my supporters." With that he turned back to his papers, and I hurried away.

The May breezes were soft, but they did us little good. We were limited to two walks a day in the palace gardens, one in the morning and one in the afternoon. All our activity was confined to a small area. Because we had suffered all winter from a lack of vegetables, we went to work digging and planting a garden. It was a relief to be outside. At first the soldiers made insulting remarks about the Tsar as a gardener, but after they saw how hard and with what good results we all labored, the taunts ended. One or two of the soldiers who had been farmers lent advice and sometimes a hand.

As spring turned into summer, the little flags of the radishes appeared. Next came the lettuce and spinach like a line of green soldiers. Soon Toma was out exclaiming with pleasure and filling her apron. Even the Empress sat outside in a chair, a blanket over her knees, cheering us on.

In the middle of July there was bad news from St. Petersburg. Lenin had tried to take the government away from Kerensky. He had failed and fled the country, but his mischief lived on. Half a million people marched to protest against the war. An urgent message came to the palace from Kerensky: "Pack and be ready to leave at a moment's notice. You are no longer safe this close to St. Petersburg."

Our fear grew as we waited to hear where we would be sent. The girls hoped it would be to their palace in the Crimea, but when Kerensky's message arrived, it was brief: "Take your fur coats and warm boots."

The Tsar and the Empress exchanged looks.

"They are sending us to Siberia," the Tsar said. We all fell silent.

CHAPTER ELEVEN

SIBERIA

Summer 1917–Spring 1918

When I was very young, I had looked forward to my eighteenth year as the year I would be allowed to go to parties. I had imagined a year filled with pleasure: ballet, theater, shopping for pretty clothes, and gossiping with friends. Instead, I would soon be on a train to Siberia. Still, when I thought of what the Tsar had lost, I could not feel sorry for myself. My seventeenth birthday came and went unnoticed. On August twelfth we celebrated Alexei's thirteenth birthday. Because the future was so uncertain, we put our worries aside and did all we could to make the day a happy one for Alexei. I made him a sailor's middy blouse from one of my own blouses. Stana sewed her best ribbons on his sailor's cap. Alexei put on his sailor's blouse and marched us up and down the halls of the palace, much to the bewilderment of the soldiers.

The next day was our last at the Alexander Palace. Though no one spoke of it, we knew we would never again see the place where we had all been so happy. The soldiers took pity on us. For the first and last time we were allowed to stroll about the park. The acres that had once been close-cropped green lawns were now a hayfield. The water in the pond was green and slimy. Still, we hardly noticed, for the pictures we carried in our minds of what had been were more real to us than the ruins that lay around us. We wandered about, seeing the happy ghosts of our younger selves everywhere. Before they returned to the palace, Stana and her sisters picked the few flowers they could find in the abandoned gardens.

"We're going to press them in our diaries," she said, "so we will always have a bit of the palace with us."

That night none of us could sleep. Mama said she would sit up with the Empress, who was not feeling well. I lay alone in our room watching the minutes and then the hours drag by on Mama's little traveling clock, which rested on the table beside my bed. The clock, a gift to Mama from the Empress, had been made by Fabergé. When it was folded up, it looked like a Greek temple, but when you opened the golden doors of the temple, there was the face of the clock with a tiny sapphire to mark each hour. Even so pretty a way to tell time could not send me to sleep.

I lay awake imagining Siberia, that empty land of endless winter. I hated the thought of being so far from St. Petersburg and from Misha. Not knowing where Misha was, we could not send him word that we were leaving. I prayed that Kerensky would let him know.

The traveling clock showed three in the morning.

For a moment I worried that everyone had left for Siberia and I was all alone. I suddenly needed to see Mama. Throwing a shawl around my shoulders, I tiptoed out of my room and down the hallway to the Empress's room, where I paused at the door, getting up the courage to knock. In the distance I heard the familiar sound of a sentry's heavy boots stamping along the wooden floors. Not wanting to be caught by him in the hallway, I hastily knocked.

"Who is it?" Mama's voice shook a little.

"It's me, Mama."

A bolt turned. The door opened, and Mama snatched me inside and locked the door after me. Mama, the Empress, and all the girls were there. Olga and Tatiana sat on the bed; Maria and Stana were cross-legged on the floor. Beside each one was a small pile of jewels glistening in the candlelight: ruby necklaces, fat and rosy pearls, glittering diamonds. They were stitching the jewels into their clothes.

"Your mama had her jewels stolen," Stana said.

"We don't want that to happen to us. We might have to live off them."

"They will expect a jewel chest," the Empress said, "and we shall have one, but our most valuable jewels will be well hidden. They belong to the monarchy, and I won't have them falling into the hands of the rabble."

The doorknob rattled. The sentry called out, "Open up in there!"

In a second's time the jewels were stuffed under pillows and carpets. There was a small closet off the bedroom. Mama pushed me and all the girls inside and closed the door on us so that we were all squashed together.

Mama opened the door slightly and said, "The Empress is unwell. I'm keeping her company. Please go away. Your presence is disturbing to her. Think what it means to her to have to leave her home tomorrow. Have a little pity."

After a moment the door closed again, and we all

burst out of the closet, gasping for breath. The rest of the night we sat there sewing the jewels into bodices and petticoats. With the first light we were finished. An hour later the carriages came to take us to the train.

The Tsar oversaw the loading of crates of his favorite wines. Several of the palace staff traveled with us: Alexei's doctor, valets, chambermaids, footmen, the Tsar's barber and the Empress's nurse, the butler and Toma and two other cooks, along with their assistants, and a sad and worried-looking Pierre, with a box full of books. I saw the looks on the faces of the palace guard as they watched the wines being loaded and all the servants climbing aboard. It seemed to me the Tsar would have been wiser to have left some of the servants and the wine behind.

So that no one would guess the real occupants of the train, and perhaps attack it in anger, the train flew Japanese flags and carried signs reading: JAPANESE RED CROSS MISSION.

The train had been made very comfortable for us. Stana and I wandered through the cars and hung out the windows to catch a breath of air on the hot August afternoons. It was when we stopped at railway stations to take on coal or other supplies that we recognized the danger we were in. The soldiers came through, shutting the blinds on the windows and sealing the cars.

Gruffly they announced, "It is for your protection."

The Empress sighed. "I can't believe the people in these towns hate us so." Still, we followed the soldiers' orders and remained hidden, not even daring to peek out at the towns we passed through. Once away from a station, we resumed our window watch. The Tsar, always thinking of how to make a geography lesson, spread out a map. As we followed the great distances—an inch on the map was three hundred kilometers—I grew sadder and sadder for the Tsar as I saw how great a country he had lost. I had fussed over losing a year of parties, but how must the Tsar feel over all his lost farms, villages, cities, rivers, and mountains? At the same time I could not help wondering how one man could make decisions for so many people.

By the fourth day, when we stuck our heads out of the train windows, we felt cool air. As far as we could see, there were kilometers of flat meadows dotted with orange and yellow wildflowers, and on the horizon the white slashes of birch tree trunks against an unending blue sky. We had reached Siberia, a land that seemed at once frightening and exciting. I knew it was a place of exile, where for years criminals and those who opposed the rule of the Tsar had been banished. Now the Tsar himself was being exiled to Siberia.

In the middle of the night the train arrived at a river town, Tyumen, nestled into the silver curl of the Tura River. We were transferred onto a steamboat whose name was *Russia*. Trailing the *Russia* were two more steamboats carrying our supplies. The small peasant villages with their neat houses slipped by like pages turned in a children's storybook. At the end of the second day we reached the village of Tobolsk. As we neared the village, we heard church bells ringing. At first we thought it was for us, but the Empress reminded us that it was a holy day, the celebration of the Divine Transfiguration. Still, we thought the pealing of the bells was a good sign.

The number of church domes on the horizon was the first thing I noticed about Tobolsk. The village's dusty streets were lined with simple wooden homes. The governor's house, where we were to live, was the only good-sized home in the whole village. This house had recently been an army barracks and was quite filthy, so we remained on the steamer while the house was put to rights. I whispered to Stana how ironic it was that the governor's house in which we would be imprisoned should be located on Freedom Street.

Our new quarters were too small for the staff. The servants had to be quartered across the street. For the first time all of us girls slept together in one room. We sat up late at night whispering to one another. We shared clothes and quarreled and comforted one another.

We were glad of one another's company, for this was a dreary place. Whatever our hardships in the palace, at least we had had familiar things around us. Here everything was strange and unfamiliar. When I looked out the window, nothing looked back at me in a friendly way.

At first we were allowed to walk about the grounds of the governor's house, but the villagers' excitement at having the imprisoned Tsar in their midst soon worried our guards. Gifts for the Tsar, cheeses and fresh eggs and sausages, began to appear on the doorstep. When we took a walk across the street to see how the servants were doing, the whole village came by to watch, many of them falling to their knees when they saw the Tsar.

Orders were given to build a tall wooden fence around the house. After that we were confined to a narrow strip of muddy ground with no flowers and no trees. The Tsar was restless. At last he summoned one of the two officials who had been sent to supervise the soldiers. "Would it be possible to have some wood to chop?" he asked.

Since they had pictured the Tsar as pampered and useless, the officials were startled, but they promised the Tsar he should have his wood. After that we saw them peeking around corners at the spectacle of the ex-Tsar of all the Russias happily chopping wood.

The wood was welcome, for the autumn was a chilly one. In a single October day the birch trees appeared to turn yellow and lose their leaves all at once. In other autumns Stana and I had gloried in the fragrance of the majestic bonfires set by palace gardeners. Now we begged the soldiers to bring us a handful of the fallen birch leaves. We made a little pile of the leaves and set them afire, breathing in the frail wisp of smoke that came from our frugal fire.

Mama and I waited anxiously for word from

Misha, but nothing came. There were rumors that Lenin was back in Russia trying to overthrow Kerensky's government and set up one of his own, but St. Petersburg was far away. The quarrels that went on among the revolutionaries seemed to have little to do with us. Still, I could not help recalling Misha's words: "If Lenin takes over, I will pray for the Tsar and his family, for they will need my prayers."

Snow began to fall. The birds, all but a flock of ravens, flew off. Our windows frosted over, closing out the world. In November we had our first taste of the Siberian winter. There was no way to keep the rooms warm. The icy wind crept through keyholes and window cracks. The water in our washstands froze. At night we piled our coats and sweaters on our beds to keep warm. We all had colds. We were all sneezing and coughing. The Empress pleaded with one of the officials to board up some of the cracks in the old house.

"There are shutters in the girls' room, but they are

stuck fast and won't close," she said.

One day at the end of November four or five workmen arrived. They were a motley lot of various ages. One of the younger ones, whose face was nearly invisible, covered as it was by a stocking cap pulled down over his forehead and a scruffy beard crawling up his cheeks, marched into our room to tackle the shutters. With nothing better to do, I lingered to watch the man. He seemed not to know what he was about. He tugged at the shutters and gave them a few random blows with his hammer. After a moment he turned around and whispered, "Close the door!"

Frightened, I was about to run for Mama when the man pulled off his cap and said, "Katya, don't you recognize me?"

I hurriedly closed the door and flung my arms around Misha. He held me tightly. When he let me go, I saw on his face the old smile, but a second later he was all seriousness.

"I managed to get leave from the army. Things are

very bad. Kerensky is defeated. It all happened in one day. They sent the ship *Aurora* down the Neva. It was flying the Bolsheviks' red flag. It fired on the Winter Palace, where all Kerensky's ministers were hiding out. Lenin and his Bolsheviks took over the railways and the bridges. The country is theirs. I was never a friend of the Tsar's, but a hundred tsars would be better than one Lenin. Now the Bolsheviks are hunting us down, getting rid of anyone who supported Kerensky. My dearest friend was brutally shot and two others are in prison. Each day the Bolshevik newspaper prints a list of those who have been executed. Each day the list grows longer."

He took my hands in his. "Katya, I must leave at once. I'm here only to warn you. I heard where you were through someone on Kerensky's staff. I have only a moment or two. I must tell you what I know, and you must tell the Tsar. Lenin means only harm to the Tsar. England has refused to take the imperial family. King George is afraid having the Tsar in England will remind his people that they, too, could have a revolution and get rid of their King.

"Katya, you and Aunt Irina must leave while there is a chance. Don't go back to St. Petersburg. The Bolsheviks have installed themselves in the mansion. It is nothing but a shambles. What's more, they are arresting the Tsar's family and friends. Tell Aunt Irina to go to The Oaks. Her people there will hide you. I'll get there as soon as I can."

"But what of the Tsar and his family?" I managed to get out. "What will happen to them?"

Misha shook his head, but before he could answer, we heard footsteps. He moved away from me only seconds before the door was flung open. "What are you doing, you lazy man?" a soldier demanded. "What's taking you so long?"

Misha said, "I'm finished, tovarich." He hurried out the door.

The moment he was gone, I rushed to Mama and the Tsar and Empress. I poured out Misha's story.

The Tsar shook his head. "It could not be worse," he said. "I was a fool to abdicate. If I had known it would be Lenin who would take my place, I would never have done it."

Although Misha said he was leaving Tobolsk at once, I stood by the upstairs windows, peering over the fence, hoping for a glimpse of him. I knew that Mama would never leave the Empress. We would have to share the Tsar's fate, whatever it was.

I thought it could not possibly get colder, but it did. Perhaps it was the chill of fear that settled over all of us. In December the temperature dropped to sixty-eight degrees below zero. Since Misha had never fixed our shutters, our room was always freezing, but we didn't dare complain to the guards or we would have given Misha away.

To take our minds off the cold, Pierre suggested we put on a play. Alexei wanted to act out a battle scene, but the Empress said, "Alexei, son, we have the war all around us. Isn't that enough?"

Pierre got out the plays of Shakespeare, and we did *Romeo and Juliet*. Alexei played Romeo, while Marie, whose golden curls had grown back, was Juliet. Olga played the nurse with a great deal of style, and the Tsar made an excellent Friar Lawrence. Stana and I were soldiers and managed a sword fight with wooden sticks. The play went well, except that Marie could not keep her eyes closed when she was supposed to be unconscious, and Alexei giggled after he drank the poison.

Because we kept busy, the cold, dark days blended one into another like the flock of ravens that seemed always to be circling the house, as if they were awaiting the death of their prey.

In spite of the cold, the Tsar insisted that we take our exercise outdoors each day. Dutifully we wrapped ourselves up in everything we owned so that we waddled rather than walked. When the weather was not quite so fierce, Alexei got the idea of building a toboggan slide.

For a week we all eagerly shoveled and patted the snow into a hill. We dragged pails of water outside and threw the water over the slide. To test it, Stana and I scrambled up to the top. From there we had a fine view of the village and waved gleefully at the townspeople. The townspeople often lingered in front of the governor's house in hopes of catching a glimpse of the Tsar, for many of them were still loyal to him. It was that loyalty that put an end to our slide.

The soldiers, seeing us waving to the townspeople, and seeing them wave back, accused us of signaling secret messages. There had been rumors of escape plans, and our careless actions made the guards suspicious. They ordered the slide destroyed. We watched helplessly as the soldiers came and tore down all our work.

Once the Bolsheviks had seized the government, there was a change in the way the soldiers treated us. The guards made suggestive remarks to us girls. They called the Empress "German spy" to her face. On one terrible day one of the soldiers actually tore from the Tsar's uniform the epaulets given to him by his father, Alexander III. The Tsar's face went deadly white, and for a moment I thought he would strike the soldier. All the rest of the day he kept to himself.

Our way of life in Siberia could not have been more simple; still, the revolutionary soldiers resented every bite that went into our mouths. Now that Lenin was in power, no money was coming to pay our expenses. By March the butcher and baker in Tobolsk would no longer extend credit to the imperial family.

A notice came from the Bolshevik government ordering the imperial family to get along on soldiers' rations. We had little but kasha, cabbage, and bread. In the cold Siberian climate it would be weeks before we could think of planting a garden.

Toma, beside herself with frustration, wailed, "Heaven help me, I never believed I would live to see the day when I would serve such slops to the Tsar."

Just when we thought nothing could be worse, the

Bolshevik government signed a peace treaty with Germany. It had grown impossible to carry out the war. The army was in chaos. The Bolsheviks had insisted that soldiers elect their own officers. Cooks became colonels and colonels cooks. There were even Bolshevik committees in the army hospitals to decide which of the wounded ought to be operated on.

We were at the dinner table when the Tsar gave us the news of Russia's surrender. He looked about at his children, shabbily dressed and bundled against the cold. He looked at the table with its frugal meal. He sank down onto a chair. "I gave up everything because I thought I would save Russia. Now a third of our country is gone, given away by the Bolsheviks." He bowed his head and covered his face with his hands.

We were all silent. All these miserable months we had turned to him for courage, and he had never failed us. If he gave up, what would become of us? Even the Empress, who was never at a loss for words or a notion of what must be done next, had nothing to say.

The girls and I looked at one another. It was Alexei who went over and put his arms around his father. "Papa, Russia has lost its land before, and we got it back."

The Tsar gave Alexei a weak smile. "You are right, my son. But my greatest worry is for what is left of our dear country. Just think—she will be ruled by the very men who have betrayed it."

I did not say a word. Though I understood how betrayed the Tsar felt, though I regretted as he did the loss of Russia's lands, I had seen what the war had done. I could not be sorry that it had ended.

While all of Russia celebrated the peace, the Tsar mourned. The treaty with Germany took away much land from Russia: Finland, Poland, the Baltic states, the Ukraine, part of the Caucasus, and the Tsar's beloved Crimea. The cold inside our hearts was as bitter as the Siberian cold outside.

In April the ice that had imprisoned the river all winter began to thaw. Along the streets the snow melted, leaving mud. Each day we left off one more sweater or cap. We began to talk of a garden. Because we had so little to eat, even the thought of fresh greens and new potatoes cheered us. But it was not to be.

Alexei fell and hurt himself, suffering a hemorrhage in his leg. The Empress was with him day and night. Just as he was beginning to recover, a mysterious man arrived from the Bolshevik government. The first day he was very polite, taking tea with us and inquiring after Alexei. The second day he informed us that "Citizen Romanov," as he called the Tsar, was to be taken away.

"My orders are to take the whole family, but that will have to wait until your son is well enough to travel." He refused to say where they were taking the Tsar.

The Empress was beside herself. "I cannot leave Alexei while he is ill, and I cannot let your father go without me," she told the girls.

The girls, seeing her misery, urged her to go with their father. "Alexei is better," Tatiana said. "I can take care of him and of the household. You must go with Papa, but you must take one of us with you."

Tatiana was the most sensible and capable, so she was chosen to stay behind and take over the care of Alexei and the house. Olga was not well, and Stana was thought too young, so Marie was chosen to go with her mother and father. The girls all clung to one another, for they had never before been separated.

It was a terrible moment when the Tsar, the Empress, and Marie were taken away in a *koshevy*. There were no seats in such a wagon. An old mattress was thrown into the wagon and covered with straw. The Tsar and the Empress went to each of their daughters, and to me, and made the sign of the cross on our foreheads, blessing us. Stana, Olga, Tatiana, and I stood hand in hand watching until the Tsar, the Empress, and Marie disappeared into cold Siberia.

Though Pierre did all he could, nothing that day would comfort Alexei. He shed so many tears, they could have filled the Neva until it overflowed.

The first letter from the Tsar and the Empress said only that they were well and not to worry. Soon after, we learned they were in the city of Ekaterinburg in the Ural Mountains. I thought anything would be better than another winter in Siberia, but Pierre appeared more worried than ever.

"I have heard bad things of that city," he said. "The Bolsheviks have taken it over. The Tsar and the Empress will find no friends there."

Tatiana urged us to keep busy. Dutifully we began to scratch out a kind of garden in the mud, but when the time came, none of us had the heart to plant seeds, for none of us, not even Tatiana, believed the Empress and the Tsar would return.

In the middle of May, on a day when the blue Siberian sky was filled with returning hawks, the official declared Alexei well enough to travel. Alexei and the girls, along with Pierre and a handful of staff, were told to pack and be ready to leave immediately. When the time for departure came, though Mama begged, she and I were not allowed to go with them.

"We are done with ladies-in-waiting" were the rough words of the commissar.

"I am not a lady-in-waiting," Mama pleaded. "I am a friend."

The commissar would not listen. I had only time to kiss Olga and Tatiana and Alexei and throw my arms around Stana. "*Proshchayte*," Stana said, breaking my heart. In a moment they were gone. When we turned to retrace our steps to the governor's house, the gates were closed to us.

"At least let us get our clothes," Mama begged.

We were given a half hour to pack.

"Where will we go, *Mamochka*?" Without thinking, I had used my childhood name for Mama.

Mama stood quietly for a moment, a bewildered look on her face. She drew herself up. With one hand she reached for her suitcase; with the other she held on to my hand. "We'll go to The Oaks."

CHAPTER TWELVE

RETURN TO THE OAKS

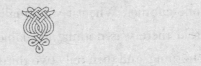

Spring 1918

Every minute of our journey to St. Petersburg, first on the steamboat and then the train, was a frightening one. Mama and I were alone. There were soldiers everywhere. We wore old clothes and tried to appear as inconspicuous as possible, but people still sent suspicious looks our way. We seemed not to be escaping danger but to be hurrying toward it.

We changed trains in St. Petersburg, where the streets were crowded with revolutionaries. Wagons passed us, heaped with furniture from looted mansions.

In the station people swarmed around the trains, trying to push their way into the cars. Parents with small children were camped out on the station floor. At the ticket windows people were mercilessly shoving one another. When it was finally our turn, we were told there was nothing available until the following morning, and then only two third-class tickets. Mama eagerly took them.

All we could get at the station restaurant was cabbage soup and tea. Though our stomachs were groaning with hunger, the look of suspicion on the faces of two guards who were watching us made us so nervous, we left half our dinner and tried to melt into the crowd. When it grew dark, we settled down on a patch of dirty floor. Next to us were a man and woman and their two small girls, who looked to be about four and five. The man stared straight ahead, lost in his own thoughts, while the exhausted-looking woman tried to manage the children, both of whom were sobbing bitterly. One little girl complained through her tears, "The bad man wouldn't let us take our dolls."

The woman sighed. "Forgive the girls," she said to us. After a searching look, which must have reassured her, she continued. "They confiscated our home. We were lucky to escape with our lives." Politely, as if we were in a drawing room instead of on the floor of a train station, she introduced herself. "I am Elizabeta Ivanova Kherna."

As the woman spoke her name, Mama eagerly grasped her hand. "I knew your sister. I am Irina Petrovna Baronova. Your sister and I were at dancing class together." The two women clung to each other like long-lost friends.

Elizabeta Ivanova looked carefully around and then whispered, "But you were a lady-in-waiting to the Empress." She leaned closer. "How is the imperial family?"

Mama told what she knew and then asked what Elizabeta Ivanova was doing there.

"It has been a nightmare. The Bolsheviks looked

the other way when the worst kind of hooligans burst into our home, taking everything. 'Rob those who robbed us!' they shouted. They got into our wine cellar and emptied the bottles down their throats. They threatened to put us on trial in our own home for exploiting the people. Andre pleaded with them." Elizabeta Ivanova covered her face and broke into tears.

The girls began to cry harder than ever. I gathered them onto my lap and asked, "Shall I make each of you a new doll?"

Their tears ended, and they watched eagerly as I poked about in my suitcase for a linen petticoat, a silk blouse, scissors, and a needle and thread. I turned the linen into heads and bodies, embroidering smiling faces on the heads. Clumsily I fashioned the silk into dresses. By the time I had finished, it was night and the two girls were asleep, each one with her doll clasped in her arms.

Mama and the girls' parents and I were too fearful
to sleep. Mama told stories of our imprisonment at the
palace and in Siberia. The Khernas told us of the
Tsar's ministers and the nobility fleeing St. Petersburg,
trying to get to Finland and then to Sweden, or, as we
were doing, to disappear into the countryside. Some of
them had been unsuccessful, ending up imprisoned in
the Peter and Paul Fortress—or worse, in front of a
firing squad. Though I said nothing, I recalled Mama's
words: "This is not France. You can be sure nothing
will happen to the great families of Russia."

When at last we parted in the morning, we were
dear friends. The girls clung to me and kissed me,
making me promise to come to see them.

The third-class car had filthy wooden benches.
Smoke and soot blew in through the windows. There
was no food. I thought of the elegance of the train that
had carried us to the front to visit the Tsar—the silk
curtains at the windows, the comfortable overstuffed

chairs, and the delicacies served to us by uniformed footmen. How little we had known of the real Russia in those days.

Though we were crowded together in the train with hardly enough room to breathe, there were no friendly exchanges. Like a rat, suspicion nibbled at all of us. Noble families were careful to disguise themselves, just as Mama and I had. In the new Russia nobility was very low indeed.

It was early evening when the train chugged to a halt at the station near our dacha. Mama and I picked up our suitcases and hurried from the train. Except for an indifferent stationmaster, the small wooden station was deserted.

Mama cautiously approached the stationmaster, a young man with bristly red hair and slits for eyes. His uniform was several sizes too large for him, so only the tips of his fingers showed at the ends of his sleeves. The Khernas had told us that the Bolsheviks had replaced all the railway personnel with their own people.

"Please, could you get us a car or a carriage?" Mama asked.

The man stared at us out of the narrow slits as if we had asked for the moon. "A car? A carriage? Where do you think you are? In St. Petersburg?"

"We need to go to The Oaks," I explained.

He looked at me for a moment with curiosity, and something that was almost sympathy. Shaking his head, he pointed at the road. "In that direction."

Mama and I picked up our bags and started out, stumbling under our burdens, for the road was nothing more than wagon ruts. I turned around once and saw the stationmaster standing there staring after us, a pitying look on his face. As the sun began to sink, it took with it the last warmth. Afraid of finding ourselves alone on the road when darkness fell, we hurried on.

At last there were the familiar landmarks: the plank bridge and then the apple orchard whose trees were covered not with the small green apples of summer, but with spring blossoms. The peasant's cottage was deserted, and no flock of honking geese ran to attack us. We seemed to be alone in the world. It was nearly dark when we made out The Oaks in the distance.

Mama stopped, puzzled, "Katya, where are the oak trees?"

They had disappeared, but worse was to come. At first we thought it a trick of the fading light, but as we drew closer, we saw that the house was a topless shell. A fire had raged through the rooms, leaving a blackened hull. The roof was gone. In the heat of the fire the glass had shattered. The empty window frames looked blindly out at us. The whole desolate ruin appeared to reproach us, as if our carelessness had destroyed it.

Mama and I held on to each other, too shocked to shed tears. Through all the frightening and miserable journey, when we were so tired we could hardly move, we had managed to think of The Oaks as a refuge. Now a giant hand had swept The Oaks away, and with it our last hope. We were too exhausted to move.

As we stood there, a man supporting himself on a cane came hobbling toward us. He stared at us for a moment as if we were figures from some picture that had suddenly come to life. "I know you," he said in a rough voice. "But why have you come back? There is nothing here for you now."

There was something familiar about the man and the angry look he gave us. It was Stepan.

"You were in the army," I said.

"Yes. I left a bit of my foot and all of my youth there." His tone was bitter.

"And Nina?" I asked.

A fleeting smile hurried over his face, quickly disappearing as if it were not at home there. "We are married," he answered shortly.

Mama seemed puzzled and impatient with our conversation. She asked, "What happened to The Oaks? Who did this?"

"Your peasants, Madame." There was an unpleasant

note of satisfaction in his voice. "They came for Vitya and Grishka, but your estate manager and his wife had already fled, probably with all your silver. When the peasants could not find them, they burned the house. They took their revenge where they could find it."

"But I never meant the peasants harm," Mama said. "How could they do such a thing to me?"

"It was not done to you," Stepan said, relenting a little, "but to Vitya. You only had the misfortune—or carelessness—to employ him." As he looked from us to our small suitcases, all the anger appeared to leave Stepan. "Where will you stay?" he asked.

When I shook my head, he said to Mama, "For now you must come and stay with Nina and me. I have not forgotten that your daughter was once kind to us."

I bent to pick up our suitcases. Mama followed slowly along behind us as if she were sleepwalking. Only once did she say anything. "Tell me," she asked, "what has become of the great oak trees?"

"The peasants came and cut them down," Stepan said. "They needed wood to keep from freezing. It was a cold winter"—he paused—"yet the heat of their anger should have been enough to warm them."

He led us to the small wooden hut, with its thatched roof. I recalled the hut from the evening I had given Stepan Nina's message. Here and there large patches of thatch were missing. A few scrawny chickens scurried about, and a swaybacked horse stood tethered to a fence post.

Stepan paused and looked around at us. Half apologetically, half tongue in cheek, he said, "I'm afraid this is not what you are used to."

"We are grateful to have any place to sleep," I said. "Last night our bed was the floor of the train station."

For the first time a look of real pity stole grudgingly over Stepan's face, as if all this time he had been fighting against it. "We will do what we can to make you comfortable," he said.

I half expected to see his mother on the chair in front of the cottage, her apron thrown over her face. As if he could read my mind, he said bitterly, "My mother died in the winter. Before I got back from the war."

The door opened, and Nina, taking the two steps in one leap, ran to embrace us. If Stepan was still resentful, Nina was all sympathy. She threw her arms about us and began to cry as if The Oaks were as much her loss as ours. "It was a terrible crime, Madame," she said to Mama. To me she said, "Oh, Miss, believe me, I tried to stop them, but they wouldn't listen. Such a waste. Everything gone. That little chair with the delicate legs and the sofa all covered in a pattern of roses. They even carried away the pictures on the walls. There was one of a garden by moonlight. When I dusted, I always lingered over that picture. I longed to step right into it and—"

Stepan interrupted her. "Now, Nina, these women

are tired and probably hungry. There will be time for talk later."

Nina apologized. "Yes, yes, what can I have been thinking?"

She led us inside. Half the room was taken up with a large stove, and arranged on and around the stove were wide wooden shelves. The floor was covered with fragrant pine boughs. The ceilings in the house were black with soot from the stove and so low that Stepan moved about with a continual stoop. An icon was hung in one corner, and a candle flickered before it. A table of rough boards and some chairs were the only furniture in the room.

"I would like to make cherry dumplings for you," Nina said. "I make very good cherry dumplings." She looked helplessly at her husband. "But I have no white flour and no butter, and it's months too soon for cherries." At that she began to cry. "We have nothing suitable to offer you, but praise to God you are alive. Terrible things have happened here. Not just at The

Oaks. Baron Nogin was lucky to escape with his life. The Bolsheviks took over his farm, and he had to flee to the Crimea."

"But why the Baron?" I asked. "He was always so good to his peasants."

"Once you begin to hate," Stepan said, "there is no stopping."

A smile brightened Nina's face. "Now sit down and just see what I have to make your tea." Nina settled Mama onto one of the wooden chairs, and I dropped beside her.

Nina pushed aside a pine bough. Beneath the bough was a trap door. She reached in and brought out a bundle wrapped in rags. When the rags were stripped away, a handsome brass samovar was revealed, shining in all its golden glory. I recognized it at once.

"When they came to burn The Oaks," Nina said, "I carried it away in an old basket. Once a week I polish it with vinegar and salt just as I used to." She filled the samovar with water and lit the coals in the burner. From behind the woodpile she produced a small container and measured out a frugal spoonful of tea into a pot, which she filled with the samovar's boiling water.

While we sipped the tea, we told our story. At each mention of the Tsar's name Nina crossed herself.

"A saint," she whispered.

"How can you utter such nonsense?" Stepan said. "The Tsar was a fool to get us into the war. It's only by God's mercy I wasn't killed along with the three million other Russians the Tsar sent to their deaths."

"Stepan!" Nina was shocked. "How can you say such things in front of the Countess?"

"All the same, I say them, and there are no more countesses. Three fourths of the men of our village were killed in the war. All the animals were stolen to feed the army. Only a broken-down horse is left to us, and we have to pull the straw from our roof to feed the poor beast."

Nina was indignant. "Stepan, that is enough. The Countess is a guest in our house." She turned to us. "You must be starving." She began to search the small cupboard, accompanying her search with groans. "No sugar, no lard. Wait. I know where the old hen is hiding her eggs." She bustled out and in a few moments was back, carrying two eggs in her apron. We had cabbage soup, and though Mama and I protested, we each had a lovely poached egg.

Nina arranged quilts on the shelves around the stove, and each of us curled up on our own warm shelf. I thought of The Oaks, a shadowy ruin, empty and desolate out there in the darkness. Where would we live? It was too dangerous to go back to St. Petersburg, where anyone connected to the Tsar was imprisoned or worse. And where was Misha? No hour passed without my wondering whether he was alive or dead.

Before I could sort out all the problems, the weariness from the journey, and from all that had happened since, spread over me like the sheltering wings of a great dark bird. I fell fast asleep, comforted by the warmth of the stove and Stepan's soft snores.

CHAPTER THIRTEEN

THE ANGEL ON THE SQUARE

Spring–Fall 1918

Mama and I ate as little as possible, but Stepan urged, "Eat up. I'm planting on your land; why shouldn't you eat our bread?" Since The Oaks had been destroyed, Stepan and the other peasants who had lived on the estate had gradually taken over its fields. "There is talk the Bolsheviks want the land," Stepan said, "but for now we'll make the most of it."

Stepan and Nina refused to allow us to help them. After watching them plowing and digging from dawn to dusk on the first day, I told them the story of the

Tsar chopping wood and the Grand Duchesses and me planting our garden. "A hundred heads of cabbage," I boasted. After that Mama and I were allowed to help.

"Katya," Stepan said, "I'll leave the feeding of old Dunka to you. The horse will appreciate your gentle touch. All the poor soul gets from me is the stick."

Having at last been given a task, I was too ashamed to tell Stepan I was terrified of horses. Pulling an armful of straw from the roof and carrying a small bag of oats entrusted to me by Stepan, I went to the shed where Dunka was stabled. He rolled his eyes at me so that the whites showed. He lifted his head and snorted a terrible snort. I cringed in a corner of the stable. We looked at each other. He was truly a poor specimen of horse, with a mangy coat, a sway-back, and all his ribs showing. In spite of myself I began to feel sorry for him.

Gingerly I reached up to run a hand over his shoulder. He shivered. Keeping as far from him as I could, I stretched out my arm, holding the bag of oats beneath his nose. He eagerly snuffed them in. The straw followed. Hanging from the wall was an old currycomb lacking several teeth. I began to comb Dunka's matted coat, keeping well away from his mouth. He stood perfectly still, making contented noises deep in his throat.

There were sore spots where his halter had bitten into his flesh.

When Stepan and Nina came into the stable, I asked, "Is there anything I could rub on Dunka's sores?"

Stepan stared at me. "With all we have to worry about, why should we worry about a broken-down horse?"

But Nina said, "Ah, Katya, you are tenderhearted. I'll make up a little poultice."

The next day Stepan let me lead Dunka while he held the plow. I trembled a little as I reached up close to the horse's mouth to grasp the halter. Dunka gave a small snort but soon was clopping along behind me.

Back and forth we went with the plow, my bare feet sinking into the soft earth. As we worked, I couldn't help but feel proud of the rows of black loam in our wake. Stepan was a different person in the field. The anger and bitterness left him. He even sang songs. At the end of the day's plowing he said reluctantly, "Dunka has never done so well. You may make a peasant yet." I grinned, for I considered that high praise coming from Stepan.

When I looked at Mama, my pleasure disappeared, for her expression was gloomy. When we were alone, she said, "What have we come to, Katya? Are we to be peasants the rest of our lives?"

"Mama, at least we are alive, and we have each other." But Mama would not be comforted.

We were both eager for news of the imperial family. I walked to the village post office to send a letter from Mama to the Empress in care of Pierre. Using the Empress's name would have given us away. No answer came back.

We did not know where to write Misha. In the evenings, when our work was finished, I wandered off to the small stream. With the croaking of the frogs and the song of a distant nightingale for company, I would tell Misha all my troubles, for I believed that somehow, wherever he was, he would hear me.

I knew that Mama and I could not continue to live on Nina and Stepan's charity. Secretly I began returning to The Oaks. The shed that had been the smithy was still standing. The forge had been carried away, but otherwise the shed was undamaged. The walls and the roof were sound. Each evening when the work was finished, I made some excuse and hurried to the shed. I bundled twigs into a broom and swept the shed out. I polished the windows to let in light. The stove that had furnished the fire for the forge was still there and would warm us when the weather turned cold.

I began to explore the ruins of The Oaks. At first it was painful to wander through the rooms where I had been so happy—the dining room, the kitchen, the parlor were nothing more than a jumble of burned wreckage. I tried to put my memories behind me. I was looking for anything that might be of use. In the kitchen I discovered a kettle and a few pans. Their handles were twisted, but they were still useful. I uncovered two chairs in the parlor. They were a little blackened, and mice had made a home in their stuffing, but otherwise they would do. I took needle and thread to the shed and cut curtains from bits of draperies that had not been entirely consumed by the fire. I salvaged a scrap of carpet for the floor and dragged an iron bedstead to the shed. One evening I dug up a bed of daisies and lilies still blooming in the garden of The Oaks and planted them at either side of the shed door.

My rummaging became an obsession. I could not wait to get away in the evenings. When Stepan wanted to know where I was going, Nina excused me, saying, "Let her be. See how much better she looks since she started her walks."

It was true. As the shed was transformed into a cottage, I began to have hope. When Stepan prophesied a good harvest, I believed we could survive the year. Beyond that, time was an endless ocean I could not see across.

Finally I told Nina my secret, for the one thing I could not find was a covering for the bed. Nina gave me a quilt, and I smuggled it into the cottage. When two of the chickens got into a fight and did each other in, we cooked them, and I stuffed two pillows with their feathers. Even Stepan was let in on the secret. He plowed a small square of land next to the cottage and gave me some seeds so that I could plant a vegetable garden.

At last it was time to take Mama to the cottage. When she first saw it, she began to cry. A moment later she was laughing. Through her laughter and tears she said, "Katya, you have created a *chudo*, a miracle. How strange, though, to see the bits and pieces of The Oaks put together." She looked about.

For the first time since we had left Siberia, her eyes lit up. "There must be other things left," she said. "I'll just look around, and then we must get peas and lettuce planted in the garden while the weather is still cool." She gave me a hug.

After we moved into the cottage, Nina came every day to see how Mama was. She tidied the tiny cottage, lingering over each broken chair or damaged table as if she were caring for the old rooms of The Oaks. Often she would bring some little treat for Mama—a jar of wild strawberry jam or a basket of wild greens she had gathered for a salad. While I was trying to put the past out of my mind, and to live like Stepan, only from one task to another, Mama and Nina seemed always to be living in the past. In Nina's eyes Mama was still the Countess Baronova. In Mama's eyes Nina was still a faithful servant.

With Mama busy with the cottage and the garden, I gave all my time to the fields. By the end of June Stepan and I had planted oats and millet and buckwheat. We put in cabbage and turnips and planted potatoes so shriveled, I could hardly believe the green sprouts that came up.

Because Dunka had taken a liking to me, I was asked to accompany him to a nearby farm, where the peasant had no horse for plowing. Stepan warned, "Pyotr is a hard master, Katya. Keep an eye on him, or he will kill poor Dunka with his beatings."

Pyotr was a square, heavily muscled man with no patience. When he first raised a stick to hit Dunka, who was too slow for him, I grabbed at his hand. The stick grazed my shoulder. I did not know where the strength came from, but in my rage I tore the stick from his hand, grabbed Dunka, and began to run away with the horse, with Pyotr after us.

"Where do you think you are going with that horse?" he bellowed.

"You can beat me all you like," I snarled back at him, "but you're not to lay a hand on Dunka. You must treat him kindly."

At that he burst out laughing. "You're a wild one. That's to my taste. Very well. You make the creature trot along with your kindness, and I'll hold back the stick."

When noontime came, I brought Dunka water and a little hay. Pyotr and I settled beneath the shade of a tree. He proceeded to wolf down a loaf of bread and a large hunk of cheese, while I made do with the bit of bread and the hard-boiled egg Nina had sent with me.

"I know all about you," Pyotr said, eyeing me suspiciously. "You had something to do with the aristocrats. We'll soon be rid of them, and a good thing. They've sucked enough of our blood."

"What do you mean?"

"My father and grandfather were serfs on The Oaks, owned like slaves."

"But that is all over. Tsar Alexander the Second freed the serfs years ago. You can't blame Tsar Nikolai for that."

"There is plenty to blame your Tsar Nikolai for.

He levied a heavy tax on us so he could pay for his palaces. If there was drought or a late freeze and we had a poor year with no money for the Tsar's taxes, they put us in jail. They auctioned off our livestock at low prices so the rich landowners like that Countess who owned The Oaks could buy them cheaply. If we pawned our clothes to get enough money to buy back one of our pigs or cows, the rich landowner sold it back to us at twice the price it was worth."

"I don't believe you," I said. "The Countess wouldn't do such a thing."

He eyed me suspiciously. "What do you know about countesses?"

"Nothing," I said hastily.

That afternoon, when I was in the field with Stepan, I told him what Pyotr had said. Stepan only shrugged. "Yes, that's all true."

"Mama would never have wanted to make it so hard for the peasants," I said.

"Ah, Katya, what did your mama know? You

came here once a year and sat on the porch and drank tea and had your little dinner parties; then you went away."

Later, when I repeated his words to Mama, she said, "I demanded what my papa had always asked, and his papa before him. The mansion in St. Petersburg and all the servants there took money. Papa said if you weren't strict with the peasants, they would cheat and steal from you." She looked down, not wanting to meet my eyes. "I was very foolish, Katya. I never thought of what the peasants suffered. How was I to know what hunger was? I only urged Vitya to send more money. I never asked how he was to get it."

June's white nights were followed by July's scorching sun. With as much excitement as I had once watched the court ball with Stana at the Winter Palace, I now watched the white blossoms of the buckwheat plants unfold and the soft green rye and millet wave in the gentle summer breeze. In our own small garden we pulled radishes to slice and eat on bread I had made myself. I often thought of Sergeant Yuri from the hospital at the Catherine Palace, who longed only to see the wheat turn golden and the buckwheat flower. I hoped he had found a place in the country.

My life fell into the simple pattern of the life peasants had always lived. I rose with the dawn, ate a crust of bread, and drank my tea. I worked in the fields until dusk with only a pause for a simple lunch. While it was still light, I fell exhausted into bed. All I knew was that I was alive. The land that made the buckwheat plants blossom and sent up a sea of grain to wave in the breeze was now our life and would be forever. I tried to put away my longing for my city of St. Petersburg. I made no plans for the future. I got up and worked and went to bed.

Our troubles were the troubles that peasants had struggled with for hundreds of years. Once a plague of grasshoppers chewed their way through part of our wheat field. Another day a hailstorm battered the rye.

There were rare days of perfect blue skies and sometimes a discovery, like the nest of a dove I found cradled in a pine tree. Tucked inside the nest were five perfect white eggs. At the end of each day I visited the nest hoping for a peek at the fledglings.

On the first day of August Mama and I celebrated my eighteenth birthday with a handful of wild blackberries on our morning bowls of kasha. After Mama gave me a kiss and her blessing, I hurried out to the field, anxious to begin work in the cool hours of the morning. As the day went on, a scorching sun filled the sky. I was hoeing a field of buckwheat, the sleeves of my blouse rolled up against the heat and my skirts hiked up for the same reason. My feet were bare. A dirty kerchief kept the dust from my hair.

On the flat land I could see a figure approaching from a great distance. Warily I put down my hoe and watched as a man made his way toward me. Strangers were rare. The man had a cap pulled down over his forehead, and his jacket was slung over his shoulder.

I knew the walk. I couldn't move.

As he came closer, Misha called out, "I'm looking for The Oaks. Can you tell me if I'm on the right road?" His look was pleasant but impersonal. I felt as if I had disappeared from the face of the earth. I began to cry. Misha looked startled, then apologetic.

"I'm sorry, Miss. Have I said something to disturb you?"

"Oh, Misha, how can you not know me?"

"Katya! Can it be true?" He pulled away my kerchief and gathered me into his arms. "I came for your birthday." He handed me a wilted bouquet of field daisies.

I couldn't stop crying. All the misery of the last months came pouring out in my tears.

At the sight of me in a stranger's arms, Stepan, Nina, and Mama had all come running. No more work was done that day. Misha walked about the ruins of The Oaks shaking his head. "In the old days at the university, when we talked of revolution, I never dreamed it would be like this." He picked up a piece of burned timber and shook his head as if the blackened and destroyed wood were the whole of the revolution.

When I showed him the cottage and the garden, he looked at me with amazement and exclaimed, "Katya, you are a wonder."

Teasing him, I said, "You no longer call me a spoiled child?"

He reached for my hand. "Katya, don't torture me with my own words."

I didn't want to worry Mama, so I waited until I had a moment alone with Misha before I dared ask, "What have you heard from Ekaterinburg? Is the imperial family well?"

The bitter look on Misha's face I had seen as he walked about the burned ruins of The Oaks returned. "You've heard nothing?" he asked. His voice was a whisper, though no one was near.

"We hear no news," I told him. "We might as well

be a thousand kilometers from St. Petersburg." I was studying Misha's face. "Something has happened, hasn't it?"

He put his hand on mine. "Lenin ordered the Tsar executed."

"It can't be! How could anyone be so cruel?" After a moment I managed to ask, "The Empress and Alexei and the girls? Are they safe?"

Misha shook his head. "No one has heard, and no one has seen them. I must tell you there is little doubt that they were executed as well. Lenin wants the Romanov family wiped out. All the Grand Dukes have been arrested and sentenced to be executed."

I left him and walked out into the field. Misha understood and did not follow me. I had lost two fathers and now my sisters as well. I sank down in the wheat and cried for the Tsar and the Empress, for Alexei, for Olga and Tatiana, for Marie and my beloved Stana, and for Russia. I cried until I had no tears left.

Days later, when I could trust myself to talk about it, I asked Misha, "How could they do such a thing?"

We were walking beside the little stream. A pale moon shone in the eastern sky, while the sun was still a circle of gold in the west. With the quiet beauty of the countryside all around us, such deeds seemed impossible.

"They are evil people, Katya. They trust no one. Lenin and his crew are like the insects that eat their own young. The very people who worked hardest for the revolution are being arrested. Kerensky had to flee the country. I was lucky to get out of St. Petersburg with my life. I thought I understood what was best for Russia. I knew too little and believed too soon."

"It's the same for me, Misha." I sighed. "I see how empty-headed I was. I understand now how hard it has been for the peasants. And remember how I turned up my nose at the poor people in St. Petersburg because they were dirty? And you said they had no water. Now we are lucky to have a bath once a week, and Mama and I share the water. There had to be changes."

I began to cry, as I did whenever I thought of the girls. "But Misha, we have traded thoughtlessness for evil."

Misha said, "As soon as I've helped you and Stepan with the harvest, I mean to go back to St. Petersburg, Katya. I know a family who will put me up. There are still a few of us left to fight against this government, in secret if we must. For however many years it takes, we will fight, until we get real freedom in Russia. If we die in the attempt, others will come after us."

As Misha spoke I began to feel a longing for my city, which was now in so much trouble. For the first time in months I let myself think of the crowds on the Nevsky, the clanging tram cars, and the reflection of the Winter Palace shimmering in the Neva. I sighed, and Misha took my hand. "Come with me," he said.

I did not ever want to be separated again from

Misha. I had lost so much. I couldn't bear to lose him too. Looking at him now, holding his hand, the only future I could imagine was one we would share. Yet I shook my head. I was afraid. At least here I was safe.

As we walked by the pine tree with the nest, I heard faint peeps. The dove's eggs had hatched. Five fledglings poked up their tiny beaks. After that I hardly let the nest out of my sight. I was resolved that no fox would steal the fledglings. I could not help but remember how the Tsar had called the girls, shorn of their curls, his fledglings. I was there at dawn, and all day long I ran in from the fields to stand watch. The last thing I did before I went to bed at night was to check the nest. But I could not be up all night. In the darkness a raccoon came, leaving behind an empty nest.

I saw that there was as little safety here as there was in St. Petersburg. I could not hide for the rest of my life. More than anything, I wanted to be with Misha. The next morning I took Misha aside. "Once Mama is settled for the winter, I'll go with you. I've talked to Stepan and Nina. Nina adores Mama, and she and Stepan have promised to watch over her. Most of the crops have done well. There will be food enough for the winter." Together we made our plans.

It was only when I came to say farewell to Mama that I nearly lost my courage. I did not see how I was to live apart from her.

"Come with me, Mama," I begged.

"Katya, I could never face St. Petersburg now. I am better here. I feel a kind of peace here at The Oaks, where I played as a child. Nina and Stepan will look after me. My greatest happiness will be in knowing that you and Misha have each other."

It was late fall when Misha and I walked out of the St. Petersburg train station and onto the Nevsky. The city welcomed us with a golden October day. We crossed Anichkov Bridge. The great bronze horses still pawed the air, but how different from the noisy, cheerful crowds of my childhood were the silent pedestrians on the prospekt with their suspicious, closed faces. Rough-looking soldiers wearing badges of the revolutionary government were everywhere. Misha took my hand, for we were both nervous walking openly in the street. Many of the stores were boarded up. Even the clanking of the trams seemed subdued.

I wanted to see the Zhukovsky mansion that had been our home. At first Misha tried to discourage me.

"It will only make you unhappy," he said.

"Perhaps it will, but I won't start my new life with my eyes closed. There has been enough of that."

We crossed the Griboedov Canal, with its perfect reflection of the domes of the Church of the Resurrection still looking like a tumble of crown jewels. There was our mansion. My heart stopped at the sight. Strung across the entrance was a crudely lettered sign that read: REVOLUTIONARY WORKERS' CENTER. I could see the yellow silk draperies fluttering from the open windows in Mama's room. I looked up at the balcony where I had stood with Misha to see the celebration of three hundred years of Romanov rule. The child who had gazed with such excitement at the golden carriage of the Tsar and the Empress was gone forever, but the city was still there.

The Neva's arms were still wrapped around St. Petersburg. The Winter Palace was surrounded with barricades and soldiers, but in the square the angel looked down at us. I thought of how Lidya had promised me, "Difficult times and even wars may come to the city, but as long as the angel watches over St. Petersburg, the city will survive."

Misha must have been thinking of the same legend, for when we turned back to the Nevsky, he was smiling.

GLOSSARY

babushka: grandma; old woman

beliye nochi: white nights of spring and summer, when it is light until the early-morning hours

borsch: beet soup

chudo: miracle

da: yes

dacha: vacation home

Duma: the Russian parliament

kasha: buckwheat groat porridge

Khristos voskres. Voistinu voskres: Christ is risen. Indeed, He has risen.

khorosho: very good

koshevy: basketlike Siberian wagon

krasivo: beautiful

kulich: Easter coffee cake

Lebedinoye Ozero: Swan Lake

Mamochka: Mommy

molodyets: well done!

nyet: no

paskha: Easter cheesecake in the shape of a pyramid

perina: featherbed

pirozhki: filled pastries

podruga: special friend

proshchayte: farewell

S rozhdestvom Khristovom: Merry Christmas

sluzhanka: female servant

tovarich: comrade

troika: carriage drawn by three horses abreast

Tsar-batyushev: little father

tsarevich: crown prince

tvorog: cottage cheese

voina: war

vorobyei: sparrow

vranyo: white lie

zabastovka: labor strike